As if the party was aware that something dramatic was taking place, they were silent.

For the moment no-one spoke.

Angela looked up at the Marquis.

He could see her face very clearly in the light from the chandeliers.

There was silence.

It was only for a few seconds, and yet to Angela it seemed as if it lasted for a long time.

Then the Marquis held out his hand.

"Thank you," he said, "I am more grateful than I can possibly say."

Angela put her hand into the Marquis's and curtsied.

She felt his fingers tighten on hers . . .

A Camfield Novel of Love by Barbara Cartland

"Barbara Cartland's novels are all distinguished by their intelligence, good sense, and good nature. . . ."
— **ROMANTIC TIMES**

"Who could give better advice on how to keep your romance going strong than the world's most famous romance novelist, Barbara Cartland?"
— **THE STAR**

Camfield Place,
Hatfield
Hertfordshire,
England

Dearest Reader,

Camfield Novels of Love mark a very exciting era of my books with Jove. They have already published nearly two hundred of my titles since they became my first publisher in America, and now all my original paperback romances in the future will be published exclusively by them.

As you already know, Camfield Place in Hertfordshire is my home, which originally existed in 1275, but was rebuilt in 1867 by the grandfather of Beatrix Potter.

It was here in this lovely house, with the best view in the county, that she wrote *The Tale of Peter Rabbit*. Mr. McGregor's garden is exactly as she described it. The door in the wall that the fat little rabbit could not squeeze underneath and the goldfish pool where the white cat sat twitching its tail are still there.

I had Camfield Place blessed when I came here in 1950 and was so happy with my husband until he died, and now with my children and grandchildren, that I know the atmosphere is filled with love and we have all been very lucky.

It is easy here to write of love and I know you will enjoy the Camfield Novels of Love. Their plots are definitely exciting and the covers very romantic. They come to you, like all my books, with love.

Bless you,

CAMFIELD NOVELS OF LOVE
by Barbara Cartland

A NEW CAMFIELD NOVEL OF LOVE BY

BARBARA CARTLAND

The Angel and
the Rake

JOVE BOOKS, NEW YORK

THE ANGEL AND THE RAKE

A Jove Book / published by arrangement with
the author

PRINTING HISTORY
Jove edition / June 1993

ISBN: 0-515-11122-8

Jove Books are published by The Berkley Publishing Group,
200 Madison Avenue, New York, New York 10016.
The name "JOVE" and the "J" logo
are trademarks belonging to Jove Publications, Inc.

PRINTED IN THE UNITED STATES OF AMERICA

10 9 8 7 6 5 4 3 2 1

Author's Note

PRIVATE theatres were built in Russia in many of the great Palaces.

The one in the Winter Garden Palace was built by Catherine the Great and can still be seen by visiting tourists.

The Peterhof Palace Theatre, built in 1745 in the reign of the Empress Elisabeth Petrovna, in place of an old riding school, was rebuilt in 1857.

It was the scene of many Gala Performances which included Ballet and Gypsy dancing, when all the streets and roads leading to the theatre would be lit up and decorated with comparable magnificence.

A large number of English Ducal houses also include theatres, which serve to provide entertainment at selected parties.

At Christmas the village children are invited to enact a Nativity Play. The audience would include those who serve in the house and work on the Estate.

Acting has always been very much a Royal pastime.

H. M. the Queen, when she was Princess Elizabeth, together with her sister, Princess Margaret, performed in Plays and Pantomimes at Christmas at Windsor Castle.

One of these was "Cinderella," with Princess Margaret in the title role and Princess Elizabeth as Prince Charming.

H. R. H. the Prince of Wales had an outstanding success when, on November 17, 1965, to crown his last year at Gordonstoun, he was cast in the role of Macbeth.

Charles II enjoyed special performances put on in the Palace of Westminster.

Sarah Bernhardt, who was staying at the same hotel as Queen Victoria at Cimiez near Nice on May 16, 1897, performed at her own request, in the Queen's Drawing Room.

Afterwards the Queen wrote in her journal:

"It is extremely touching, and Sarah Bernhardt's acting was quite marvellous, so pathetic and full of feeling."

chapter one

1892

ANGELA Brooke knocked at the door of the small cottage.

It was opened by a girl of about ten.

" 'Marnin', Miss," she said when she saw who was outside.

"How is your Mother?" Angela asked.

"She's 'ad a good night, Miss, but th' twins be that 'ungry she don' know 'ow she can cope wi' 'em!"

Angela gave a little laugh as she walked down the narrow passageway towards the bedroom of the cottage.

On the bed in the sparsely furnished room was a woman holding one baby in her arms while the other lay beside her.

"Good-morning Mrs. Marsh," Angela said. "I hear you have had a good night."

"I'm all right, Miss Angela," the woman on the

1

bed replied, "but these boys was shoutin' at Oi soon as dawn broke for more milk than Oi can give 'em."

Angela put a parcel down on the bed as she said:

"I have brought you something for that. Mama always said that the best thing to produce milk was yeast, so I called at the Brewers yesterday and they gave me a big pot of it."

"That sounds strange," Mrs. Marsh remarked.

"It does not taste very nice," Angela said, "but, try and take it, otherwise the twins will suffer and I can see they are going to be big, strong boys, just like Ben."

"That's wot Oi 'opes," Mrs. Marsh replied. "But if they goes on as they are now, they'll eat us out o' 'ouse and 'ome!"

She laughed at her own joke.

Angela, having put the yeast she had brought beside the bed, opened the parcel.

"I looked through what Mama always called 'The Baby Box' last night," she said, "and I found a shawl and two little woollen coats which the twins can wear until they get too big for them."

"That's real kind o' you, Miss Angela," Mrs. Marsh exclaimed. "You're an Angel from 'eaven— that's what you are—and there's no one in t'village wouldn't say th' same!"

Angela smiled.

She was used to being told that she was an Angel.

It was the reason she had been christened Angela, which she knew was derived from the Greek word "Angelos."

She remembered her Mother telling her how,

when she was born, she looked so pretty that both the Nurse and the Doctor had exclaimed:

"She is like an Angel, Lady Brooke, and no one could ask for more when they have a child."

"I never have asked for more," Angela's Mother had said softly, "and you have looked like an Angel and been like one ever since you arrived."

"That is the nicest thing you could say to me, Mama," Angela had replied, and kissed her.

It was sad that her Mother was not alive.

She knew how interested she would have been in knowing that Mrs. Marsh, who already had five children, had now produced twins.

It was going to make the difficulty of feeding her family worse than it was already.

Angela wished, as she had so often before, that they could employ more men on the Estate.

But, if things were difficult for the Marshes, it was also very difficult for her and her brother Trevor to keep their heads above water.

She left the Marshes' cottage and walked back through the village.

She then started up the long drive towards the Priory.

As she went, Angela was worrying.

It was something she did consistently these last months because, when her brother was in London, she was left to cope with all the complaints and difficulties at home.

Only this morning, before she had gone to the village, the gardeners had told her they needed more tools.

She knew if they did not have them, it would

be impossible for them to provide the house with vegetables.

Also the tools were essential to keep the rest of the garden tidy.

It was ridiculous, she knew, to expect only two men, who were getting old, to do so much.

In her Father's day they had eight gardeners, most of whom were young and active.

Since her brother had inherited the Baronetcy, things seemed to have gone from bad to worse every year.

She was not jealous of Trevor being in London.

She felt she could hardly complain, as all his friends were there.

But it was very dull in this part of Hertfordshire, where she saw few people.

She first struggled to try to keep the Priory as comfortable as it had been in her parents' day.

Yet she knew it was a hopeless task!

They had only one old couple to look after a house consisting of thirty bedrooms, huge Sitting-Rooms, a Picture Gallery, and a Library.

There was also the Hall, where originally the Monks had sat at a long refectory table.

It was there that they had welcomed every traveller, and nobody was ever turned away unfed.

The Brookes had come into possession of the Priory after the Dissolution of the Monasteries by Henry VIII.

Then it had laid empty until Queen Elizabeth came to the throne.

She had had no intention of restoring the Priories and Monasteries to their original owners.

Therefore, they became presents which she gave to those who had served her well.

The Brooke who had received the Priory and the Estate in which it stood had been a sailor and a friend of Sir Walter Raleigh's.

He had retired with many honours and a sum of money that seemed to him a fortune.

He had been succeeded by his son.

It was later that a Baronetcy was given to the Brooke who lived at the Priory.

Angela's brother was the 9th Baronet and exceedingly proud of his ancestry.

Unfortunately, it did not provide him with the money that was needed to keep up the Priory and the Estate.

It was therefore becoming, Angela thought miserably, more and more dilapidated.

It still looked very beautiful from a distance.

Yet, as Angela knew only too well, it was desperately in need of repair.

Part of the roof leaked and the ceilings in two of the State bedrooms had fallen down.

The diamond-paned windows had lost a great deal of glass, and the rooms themselves were crying out for paint.

Angela walked on.

As she saw the sun shining on the Priory, she thought, as she had often done before, that it was unconquerable.

It had stood for so many years.

It had survived the invasion of Cromwellian troops who had killed the Brooke of the time because he was a Royalist.

5

It had flourished during the Restoration of King Charles II, but had sunk into neglect in the reign of Queen Anne.

This was because the Brooke who owned it then was fighting under Marlborough and had no time to attend to his possessions.

The Priory had luckily flourished under their Grandfather.

He had, as a young man, inherited a large and unexpected fortune.

He had spent a great deal of his money on the Priory and the land.

But like so many other rich men, he had thought his money would last for ever.

In the last few years of his life he had to make vast economies.

Fortunately, at the time when Angela's Father had inherited, he had been married to an heiress— not because she was rich, but because he loved her.

The Priory blossomed once again.

Everybody who visited it would exclaim at its beauty and the comfort they found there.

Then, when Angela's Mother died, the money that she and her husband had spent so lavishly died with her.

Her Father had five sons and three daughters.

He had left his vast fortune so that if one of his children died, the others would inherit their money.

It took Angela's Father some time to realise how poor they now were.

However, it was her brother who had to face the grim truth that he had very little money and what there was would not be sufficient to keep up the Priory.

He had gone to London determined somehow to earn some sort of income.

However little it might be, it would contribute towards their food and to the upkeep of the Prioriy itself.

"How can we have let it get into the state it is in now?" Trevor asked Angela despairingly the last time he was home.

She did not bother to answer.

They both knew that if one owned a large house without being able to care for it properly, it would fall into disrepair.

It got worse year by year and month by month.

It was the Priory that had eventually driven Trevor to London.

"I will find something to do," he said confidently. "I have a great number of friends there who were with me at Eton and Oxford who I am sure will help me if they can."

He did make a little money, and Angela thought it very clever of him.

One rich man wanted a number of horses which Trevor had been able to provide.

He made a small commission for himself over the deal.

Another wanted a house that was large enough so that he could entertain.

But it must be near enough to London for him to return to it at night after enjoying a good dinner.

It had taken a little time to find it.

Finally Trevor had discovered exactly what his

friend required and again received a commission on the purchase.

Angela could not help regretting that so much of what he made had to be expended on staying in London.

Although his lodgings were cheap and not very comfortable, they seemed expensive to her.

As she drew nearer to the Priory, she could see that one of the windows on the top floor had fallen forward.

This must have happened yesterday.

She wondered if old Higgins, who was the only man in the house, would be able to repair it.

If she asked the Carpenter to come up from the village, it would cost money.

She thought it unlikely, however, that Higgins would be able to do it, as he was suffering from rheumatism.

He was finding it difficult even to carry a tray.

He was not likely, therefore, to be able to use the tools that would be required for the job.

She remembered the old days when there were four young footmen in the Hall.

At least one of whom would have made short work of nailing back the window.

Now the footmen were gone.

Their uniforms with their crested silver buttons and white breeches were stored up in the attics.

As she remembered the attics, she thought she should go up and check to see if everything was all right.

She had neglected them for over a month and the rain had seeped in through a hole in the roof.

It had damaged some curtains which had been stored there when her Mother had replaced them with a better and more expensive velvet.

The curtains had not been wanted.

But Angela had wondered if they were not better than a number of those that covered the windows now.

Some of them had become torn and were badly faded.

Because she knew she must do something about the window, she hurried up the last part of the drive.

She reached the court-yard in front of the huge oak door.

It had stood there since the Priory was built.

Angela often thought it was a Herculean feat for Higgins to open it in the morning, as it was so heavy.

It was open now, and Angela walked inside.

As she did so, she saw, lying on the refectory table, a top-hat.

She stared at it for a minute, then gave a little cry.

The hat had not been there when she left, and she knew that Trevor had come home.

She ran into the Hall and along the corridor which led to the small Drawing-Room in which they habitually sat.

"Trevor! Trevor!" she called.

"I am here, Angela."

She burst into the room and saw her brother standing at the window.

He was looking out at the rose-garden, in the centre of which was a sun-dial.

He turned, held out his arms, and she ran towards him.

"You are . . . home!" she said breathlessly. "How . . . exciting! Why did you . . . not let me . . . know you were . . . coming?"

He kissed her on both cheeks, then held her at arm's length to look at her face before he said:

"You are looking very lovely—in fact exactly like an Angel!"

"What are you talking about?" Angela laughed. "I look as I always do. But you look very smart! I am sure that is a new coat."

Sir Trevor appeared a little shame-faced.

"It is," he replied, "but I must have some decent clothes to wear, although in fact I have not yet paid for it."

"Oh, Trevor!" Angela exclaimed. "How . . . could you! You know there is no . . . money in . . . the Bank."

"That is something about which I want to talk to you," her brother replied.

Angela looked at him apprehensively.

Then she said quickly:

"Does Mrs. Higgins know you are here? Although goodness knows what there is to eat for luncheon."

"It does not matter," Trevor said vaguely. "I expect she will find something."

Angela was worried.

It was unlike her brother to be so casual about anything so important to him as his food.

She was sure something disastrous had happened about which she had not yet learnt.

At the same time, she thought that Trevor was looking exceedingly handsome.

He had obviously ridden home, because he was wearing riding-breeches and highly polished boots.

She wondered what sort of horse he had put in the stable and if there would be a chance of her riding it.

She missed, more than she ever dared say, the horses she had ridden when her Father was alive.

"I want to talk to you, Angela," Trevor was saying, "and whether you are surprised or shocked at what I have to tell you, I think you will agree that it is something worth considering."

"Now you are frightening me!" Angela said. "What has . . . happened? What are you . . . talking about?"

Trevor moved from the window, where they had been standing, and walked to the fireplace.

It had a finely sculpted marble mantelpiece which had been added to the house in the previous century.

His head and shoulders were reflected in the mirror which stood over it.

The frame was carved by Chippendale.

Angela had always thought it was one of the most beautiful mirrors in the house.

Some of the mirrors, although not as good as this one, had been sold.

It had been an unspeakable agony for both Trevor and herself when they had had to sell anything.

"These things have survived all down the centuries!" Trevor had said angrily. "It is sacrilege that we should have to part with them now! They should belong to my sons, my sons' sons, and the generations who come after them."

"I know, dearest," Angela agreed, "but if you starve to death, you will have no sons to follow you and this particular pair of mirrors will not be missed, as they are in one of the rooms we seldom use."

She knew this was cold comfort.

She knew by the expression in her brother's eyes and the tightness of his lips that he wanted to rage at Fate.

He hated to part with anything in the Priory.

As he said, they belonged to the Brookes who were not yet born.

Trevor waited for her to settle down before he began talking.

She seated herself on the sofa.

As she did so, she thought that it needed a new cover, as the one she was sitting on was threadbare in places.

"I expect," Trevor began as if he were addressing an audience, "that you know what I mean by 'the Gaiety Girls,' and the success they have been in London?"

"You have told me about them from time to time," Angela answered, "and I only wish I could see them!"

Trevor hesitated for a moment before he said:

"That is something you will be able to do if you will agree to what I am going to suggest."

Angela looked at him in astonishment.

This was something she had certainly not expected him to say.

She often thought that the stories of the Gaiety Theatre and the Girls who performed there were like fairy-tales.

Because they obviously interested Trevor, and because she was curious, she pressed him when he was home to tell her about the Shows that took place.

Besides, the costumes of the Girls who captivated every man in London.

"How would it be possible for me to see the Girls of the Gaiety Theatre," she asked, "unless you intend to take me to a performance?"

She thought this was unlikely, and even if he did so, she had nothing to wear.

"You have heard me talk of George Edwardes," Trevor replied.

Angela had the feeling that he was choosing his words with care.

"Yes, yes," she agreed. "I remember you telling me how clever he had been in realising a long time ago that Burlesque was finished and how he had introduced Musical Comedy."

Trevor nodded.

"Yes, that is what I told you," he said, "and also that the new Shows are an amazing success and every man in London flocks to see them."

He laughed before he added:

"They say that men will spend every penny they possess in waiting at the Theatre in order to take a Gaiety Girl out to supper and often have to walk home because their pockets are empty."

Angela thought this was a stupid thing for any man to do.

She knew, however, it would be a mistake to say so.

She was longing for her brother to get to the point of the story and where it affected her.

"I went to the Gaiety last night," Trevor continued, "and went round after the Show."

"Round where?" Angela asked.

"To the Stage-Door, of course!" her brother said sharply. "Actually, I was picking up one of the actresses, as we were going to a supper-party at Romano's."

Angela looked at him questioningly, and he said quickly:

"I was not paying—I was a guest—and a very good party it was too!"

As if her brother were aware she thought he was being extravagant, he said:

"I promise you, Angela, I am spending as little as I possibly can, but just occasionally I have to entertain my friends."

There was something slightly aggressive in his voice now, and Angela said quickly:

"Yes, of course, Dearest, I know how careful you are."

"When I went back-stage," Trevor went on as if it were a relief not to have to talk about himself, "I found George Edwardes in a terrible tizzy."

"Why? What had happened?" Angela asked.

"A party had been arranged for this weekend at the house of the Marquis of Vauxhall. You have heard me talk about him?"

"Yes, you told me what marvellous horses he has," Angela agreed.

"Well, he invited me, which I thought was jolly decent of him," Trevor said, "and George Edwardes had agreed that six of his Girls should be there on Saturday night."

"To stay with the Marquis?" Angela asked in astonishment.

"Yes," Trevor said, "but for a very particular reason."

"And what is that?"

"The Marquis, and I do not think I have told you this before, fancies himself as a playwright."

"Do you mean—for the Theatre?"

"Of course I mean for the Theatre!" Trevor snapped. "He has a Theatre of his own. He got the idea from the one the Tsar of Russia has in the Winter Palace in St. Petersburg, but his is even bigger and more impressive."

"He must be very rich to own his own Theatre!" Angela remarked.

"Of course he is rich!" Trevor answered. "He is so rich that he can have anything he wants, and although it seems extraordinary, he enjoys writing Plays that are performed for his guests when he gives a party."

Angela thought it sounded rather strange.

She knew that most of her brother's friends had up till now been more concerned with their horses than anything else.

"The Marquis had everything fixed for a performance on Saturday evening," Trevor went on. "But George Edwardes had only just learnt that Lucy Lucas, who was to play the most important part, had collapsed with a high temperature."

"How annoying for the Marquis!" Angela said. "I suppose it will spoil the Play."

"Of course it will," Trevor said, "and if there is one thing the Marquis dislikes more than anything else, it is having his arrangements upset."

"But, surely, Mr. Edwardes can find him somebody else to take her place? You told me there was a number of Girls in the last Play."

Angela paused, trying to recall the name.

Then she added:

"Is it not called 'Cinder-Ellen Up-to-Date'?"

"Yes, that is right," her brother agreed, "but you see, Lucy, who was to take the part, was the only Girl at the Gaiety who really looked like an Angel."

"Like an Angel?" Angela replied. "How extraordinary! Why should the Marquis want an Angel on his stage?"

"Because he has written a Play which is based on 'The Rake's Progress,' " her brother answered. "You must have seen the drawings by Hogarth?"

"Yes, of course I have," Angela agreed. "They are all in one of the books in the Library."

"Well, he has made 'The Rake's Progress' his theme and the Angel saves the Rake at the end— or something like that."

"I think that is a clever idea," Angela enthused. "After all, it was very sad to think of a man sinking deeper and deeper into debauchery until he dies."

"As the Angel, according to George Edwardes, is essential to the Show, he knew that the Marquis would be furious if Lucy could not turn up."

"So what is he going to do about it?" Angela asked.

16

"He had no idea," her brother answered, "and as I spoke to George Edwardes, he said:

" 'I would give a thousand pounds to prevent this happening.' "

"A thousand pounds!" Angela gasped. "Then it must certainly be a serious situation."

"It is," Trevor replied, "and I told him that for a thousand pounds I could provide him with an Angel who would satisfy the Marquis's requirements."

There was silence while Angela stared at her brother.

Then at length she asked:

"What . . . are you . . . saying? What are you telling me?"

"I am telling you," her brother replied, "that for a thousand pounds, and God knows we need it, you must play the part of the Angel in the Marquis of Vauxhall's Theatre!"

"You must be crazy," Angela said, "how can I possibly do such a thing?"

"Why not?" Trevor argued. "You have been told often enough that you look like an Angel, and it is actually true. And the only thing you have to do is learn one or two lines and do what the Marquis tells you. It should not be difficult."

"But . . . it is impossible!" Angela said.

"Why?" her brother demanded. "You used to fancy yourself doing the Charades we played when Mama was alive, and I remember how four or five years ago you took part in a Nativity Play which Mama produced in the village."

"But . . . that was different," Angela said.

"Why is it different?" her brother asked. "All you have to do is to walk onto the stage, looking like yourself, and say whatever the Marquis says you have to say."

"B-but . . . how can I possibly . . . go to this house . . . and besides . . . I have no clothes—"

"That is no trouble," Trevor interrupted. "George Edwardes will provide these and, incidentally, I told him you would do it."

Before his sister could speak, he added quickly:

"At least I said to him that I could find him an Angel who could fill the bill as well as if not better than Lucy. But I did not tell him I was thinking of my sister."

"Why not?" Angela asked.

Her brother looked away from her before he replied:

"Let me explain. If you go to the Marquis's, you go as a Gaiety Girl provided for the occasion by George Edwardes. It would be totally incorrect at that sort of party for you to go as yourself."

"What do you mean by 'that sort of party'?"

Angela thought her question had embarrassed her brother, and there was a long pause before he said:

"You cannot be so stupid as not to know that as a Lady, you cannot associate with Gaiety Girls, even though some of them are very respectable."

He paused and then continued:

"In fact, one to whom I have spoken is the daughter of a Parson."

"In which case," Angela asked, "why should anybody be shocked if I take part with them in a Play?"

Her brother sat down on the sofa beside her.

"Now, listen, Angela," he said seriously, "you have to trust me to know what is right and what is wrong."

He smiled at her, then continued:

"It would be very wrong for you, as Papa and Mama's daughter, to be hob-nobbing with Gaiety Girls and staying at the house of the Marquis of Vauxhall!"

"Why should it not be right if they are staying there?" Angela asked.

Trevor put his hand up to his forehead as if he were seeking for an explanation.

"It would be embarrassing for him, embarrassing for you, and would undoubtedly upset the Gaiety Girls," he said finally.

Angela digested this before she said:

"I think I understand. Then who am I supposed to be?"

"I will think of a name for you," Trevor said, "but it will not be mine! You will do it?"

"I . . . I shall be very frightened," Angela admitted. "At the same time—a thousand pounds! Oh, Trevor, think what we could do to the Priory if we had that money!"

"That is exactly what I was thinking," he said, "although I should have to keep a small part of it in order to settle some of my bills."

"But not too much," Angela said, "and a thousand pounds, if we are careful, will go a long way to making things look as beautiful as they were when Mama was alive."

"I was thinking of that all the way here," Trevor

remarked. "But we must get busy, and now that you have agreed, I think we should go back to London to-night."

"To-night?" Angela repeated in astonishment.

"There is a lot to be done," Trevor answered. "George Edwardes will provide you with clothes, but of course you first have to try them on, and they have to make you look like an Angel, not like an ordinary Gaiety Girl, or the Marquis will not be pleased."

"Why are you so frightened of him?" Angela questioned.

"The answer to that is simple," her brother replied. "George Edwardes is looking to him to help finance the next Show he is putting on, which I gather is going to be an expensive one, and I hope to have the opportunity of riding his horses."

He paused and then continued:

"Also, I have the feeling he might give me a commission for finding one or two Polo ponies he requires."

Trevor saw that his sister was listening, and went on:

"He said something about it the other night, but I did not get a chance to say I could help him."

"Then I do see that I am very important," Angela said.

"The important thing is that we will get a thousand pounds," Trevor replied, "and I am only hoping we can increase it while we are at Vaux."

"Is that the name of the Marquis's house?"

"It is," Trevor replied. "Do you never read the newspapers?"

"Only when we can afford them," Angela said somewhat apologetically.

Her reply made her brother look a little shamefaced, as if he had forgotten how poor they were.

"And now that is agreed," she said, "I will go and see what Mrs. Higgins can give you for luncheon and pack up what clothes I have to take to London."

She paused before she asked:

"By the way, how are we going? I thought you had ridden down."

"I meant to, but when I reached the stables, I saw a Chaise and hired it."

"I am sure it was very expensive!" Angela exclaimed. "Who will pay for it?"

"George Edwardes," Trevor said. "I made it clear to him that the Lady I had in mind lived in the country and I would have to rush down to see her and persuade her to come back with me."

Angela looked at him and said slowly:

"You were quite certain from the very beginning that I would do what you wanted!"

"I was quite certain that you would not turn down a thousand pounds with which to improve the Priory!" he replied.

"I have to agree with you there," Angela said, "but, please, Trevor, if you have anything in your pocket, will you give it to the Higginses? We have not paid them their wages for weeks!"

"We can afford to now that the 'Golden Fleece' is almost within our grasp."

Angela gave a little cry.

"Do not boast, but Touch Wood!" she exclaimed.

21

"Oh, Trevor, supposing I make a terrible mistake and you are ashamed of me?"

"You have nothing to do except look like an Angel," he said firmly. "Get that into your head. The less you say and do, the better!"

Angela laughed.

"You are not very complimentary!"

"To tell you the truth," her brother admitted, "I am very frightened too. If anyone has the slightest inkling that you are my sister, I shall be in the 'Dog-House'!"

"As bad as that?" Angela enquired.

"You know as well as I do what the Family would say and how shocked they would be at the very idea of you associating with women who paint their faces and prance about on the stage, where they are stared at by anybody who can pay the price of a seat."

Angela thought of their elderly aunts and knew that Trevor was speaking the truth.

"You are quite right," she said, "and I will be very, very careful. I will tell the Higginses that I am going to stay with one of our cousins."

She suddenly thought of something.

"I suppose you have somewhere for me to go in London before we set out for the Marquis's house?"

"I have arranged something," Trevor said, "but, again, you must not talk about it."

"Who shall I talk to?" Angela asked. "The frogs in the lake . . . the birds in the trees? You know as well as I do that I can be here for weeks at a time and speak to no-one!"

"There are the people in the village," her brother

remarked, "and we do not want them to talk either. Is there anything to drink?"

She knew by the way he spoke that he was very relieved, although he did not say so, that she had agreed to do what he wanted.

But she had the feeling that there was more to the story than he had told her.

Perhaps in some way he was involved in the Marquis's Play being a success.

She knew of old, however, that it was a mistake to ask her brother too many questions.

She merely replied:

"You can look in the cellar, but I think you had the last bottle of claret when you were here three weeks ago."

"I will go and have a look," Trevor said. "In the meantime, there is no need for you to pack a whole lot of things. I will see that George Edwardes dresses you as soon as you set foot in London."

"He must be very impressed by you!" Angela remarked.

"On the contrary," Trevor contradicted, "he is impressed by the Marquis, impressed with his money, and terrified of losing his patronage. That is a very different thing."

He went from the Sitting-Room, as he spoke, and Angela heard him walking along the passage towards the cellar.

She put her hands up on each side of her face and shut her eyes.

How could she possibly do what Trevor asked without making a mess of it?

'I am crazy to listen to him!' she thought.

Then, almost as if it were there in front of her eyes, she could see the thousand pounds which George Edwardes would give him if he produced an Angel.

A thousand pounds would repair the roof, the ceilings, and the windows.

It would pay the bills they owed in the village and the wages for which the Higginses were waiting.

"Of course I must do it!" she told herself. "How can I possibly refuse?"

And yet, as she went upstairs to her bedroom, she thought that what lay ahead was very frightening.

It was like stepping out from something that was familiar into a world of torment.

She walked across the room to look into the mirror.

Did she really look like an Angel?

Supposing when George Edwardes saw her he was disappointed, or told Trevor he had found someone better?

Then she knew she would be very stupid if she did not realise that she looked exactly like everybody's idea of an Angel.

It was the impression she had given people ever since she was in the cradle.

"Ain't she pretty? Just like an Angel!" she could hear people saying to her Mother.

"You're an Angel from Heaven—that's wot you are!" Mrs. Marsh had said only an hour or so ago.

Her complexion was certainly very clear and translucent.

Her eyes were the blue of a summer sky.

Her small, straight nose and Cupid's-bow mouth distinctly resembled those of the Angels in the pictures her Mother had shown her when she was a child.

Her hair was the soft gold of the sun that rose in the sky.

It had not darkened since she had been born, which was surprising.

And yet the long lashes which curled upwards like a child's had grown a little darker.

She looked very young, very pure and, in a way, very spiritual.

It was not something she expressed to herself, but she had always prayed that she was as good as her name.

She turned from the mirror, knowing that time was passing and they had not yet had Luncheon.

She knew that Trevor would be agitating to leave.

"I must pack," Angela told herself.

Then, as she opened her wardrobe, she thought how shabby she would look in London.

Undoubtedly the gorgeously dressed Gaiety Girls would look down on her.

'Perhaps they will not see me until I am dressed as they are,' she thought hopefully.

She began to put her things into a small trunk.

As she did so, she was aware that her heart was beating frantically and her lips were dry.

Whatever Trevor might say, however reassuring he might sound, she was taking a leap in the dark.

She had no idea where she would land.

chapter two

By the time Angela came downstairs, Trevor had eaten a quick meal and brought the Chaise round to the front-door.

She saw it was an up-to-date and expensive one.

The two horses that were pulling it were, she knew, well bred.

"Come on," her brother said, "you have been a long time!"

Angela thought this was unfair, considering no-one else could have been quicker.

Old Higgins was standing in the Hall, and she said to him:

"I know you and Mrs. Higgins will look after everything. I do not expect to be gone for more than two or three days."

"It's nice for you to have a change, Miss Angela," Higgins replied.

He dropped his voice before he added:

"Sir Trevor's given me some money towards our wages and for food."

Angela smiled.

She knew that was more important than anything, and she hated to think of the Higginses going hungry because it embarrassed them to have to ask for more credit in the village.

"I am sure things will be better in the future," she said optimistically.

She ran down the steps, and Higgins followed her slowly with her trunk.

It was only a small one.

Angela had carried it downstairs rather than ask Higgins, with his bad legs, to come up for it.

Higgins put it on the back of the Chaise and strapped it down.

Trevor waited impatiently, and Angela knew that he was longing to get away.

At last Higgins said:

"That should hold fast, M'Lady, 'til y' reaches London."

"Good-bye!" Trevor called, and the horses moved forward.

As they went down the drive, Angela could hardly believe that she was leaving home and going off on a strange adventure.

She knew it was no use complaining to Trevor when she had so often told him how dull it was in the country without him.

What was more, she had longed to go to London.

It would, however, have been different if she had been going as a *débutante* as should have happened last year if her mother had not died.

She would have been presented at Court and perhaps be given a Ball.

To-day they were without the money her mother had provided, and the little her Father had left them was spent.

Her aunts, too, were almost as poor as she and Trevor were.

It was, however, something she did not want to speak about at the moment.

She sat back in the comfortable padded seat.

It was a joy to be driving along the lanes, where the hedgerows were a bright green.

The wild primroses and daffodils were growing in the grass beneath them.

Because she so seldom got away from the Priory, it was lovely to pass by the woods.

There were also great grey-stone Norman Churches as they hurried through the small villages with their thatched cottages.

Trevor did not speak.

He was too intent on driving his horses as quickly as he could.

Angela wanted to ask why they were in such a hurry.

Then she remembered there were clothes to be provided for her.

Perhaps there were other things to find or learn about before they left for the Marquis's house.

She tried to remember where Vaux was and had the idea it was not far from London.

Because he was such an important race-horse owner, she thought it might be on the way to Newmarket.

She glanced at her brother and thought that while he was looking very smart and handsome, he was also worried.

She was afraid if she asked the question, he would say he was worried about her.

'I must be very, very careful to do what he wants,' she told herself.

She was terrified that somehow, and it would be her fault, he would not receive the thousand pounds he had been promised.

It took them only two hours to reach London.

As they began to find houses on either side of the road and there was quite a large amount of traffic about, Trevor said:

"I am going to take you to my Lodgings."

"That is exciting," Angela said. "I have always longed to see them."

"It is something you should not do," he said, "but there is nowhere else we can go without having to make explanations as to why you have come to London, and naturally I do not want anybody to see you."

Angela looked at him in surprise.

"Why not?" she enquired.

"Because, as I have told you, you are going to the Marquis's house not as yourself, but just as a girl I happen to know who is of no particular consequence and comes from a middle-class family."

Angela stared at him in astonishment.

"From a middle-class family?" she exclaimed. "Why should I be that?"

"Because otherwise it would be impossible for you to stay at Vaux with the Girls from the Gaiety."

"You mean that no one in Society would accept them?" Angela asked, working it out in her mind.

"Of course I mean that," Trevor said, "and do be sensible, Angela. If anybody knew that I was using my sister to get a thousand pounds from George Edwardes, I would be socially ostracised, and might even be turned out of my Club."

Angela gave a cry of horror.

"As bad as that? Oh, Trevor, do not let us do it! Supposing I let you down and all those terrible things happen?"

"You know as well as I do that we need the money," Trevor said. "It is very difficult for me to earn that amount. I assure you, I have tried and tried, and for the last month I have failed to receive as much as a penny!"

He spoke bitterly, and Angela laid her hand on his.

"I know you have tried," she said in her soft voice, "and it is very clever of you to make as much as you have. I promise I will be very careful."

"You have to be," Trevor replied, "and you do understand that at the Marquis's party, you are—my friend."

He paused before the last word, and Angela thought he was about to say something different.

Then she asked:

"Do all the men whom the Marquis invites bring a friend with them?"

"Not all of them," Trevor answered, "and the five Girls from the Gaiety are already attached to the special friends of the Marquis."

Angela thought this over.

Then she said:

"Is it what the French would call a *chère amie?*"

"Yes," Trevor said briefly.

Angela was not quite certain what being a *chère amie* meant or what happened if one became such a person.

She thought Trevor would be annoyed if she asked him too many questions.

They therefore drove on in silence.

They reached Half Moon Street, which led off Piccadilly.

It was a narrow street with a number of tall houses on either side of it.

"This is where I have my Lodgings," Trevor said, "and you understand, Angela, they are essentially for Gentlemen."

Angela did not reply, and he went on:

"If they are visited by women—they are not called Ladies."

"I am sure nobody will know," Angela replied, "and if anyone should come to see you, I will hide."

"That is certainly something you should do," Trevor agreed.

He drew the horses to a standstill outside a house at the end of Half Moon Street.

He got out and knocked on the door.

It was opened almost immediately by an elderly man whom Angela thought must be the Porter.

"Is Atkins upstairs?" Trevor asked.

"Aye, Sir Trevor," the Porter said. "D'ye want me to fetch 'im?"

"That would be very kind of you," Trevor replied. "I do not want to leave the horses."

The Porter hurried up the stairs and Trevor went back to the Chaise.

He had given Angela the reins when he had got out.

She was having no trouble, however, as the horses were tired, having made two long journeys.

While they were waiting, Trevor unstrapped her trunk from the back of the Chaise.

He did not lift it down, but looked towards the door.

It was then a man appeared who was quite obviously, Angela thought, exactly as she imagined a Gentleman's valet would look.

" 'Evenin', Sir Trevor," the man said. "I was expectin' you about now."

"I told you when I would arrive," Trevor said. "Take this trunk upstairs."

"I 'opes it's not 'eavy!" Atkins said with a grin.

He picked it up, and Trevor walked to Angela's side.

"I want you to see my Lodgings," he said in a loud voice, "so, while I take the horses to their stable, I suggest you go up with my valet."

He paused, and then continued:

"He is carrying up the clothes I collected when I was in the country. I will join you as quickly as I can."

Angela knew from the way he spoke that he was speaking so that the Porter would hear what he said.

Wanting to play her part as Trevor expected her to, she said:

"I will be very interested to see your Lodgings, and perhaps later you will take me to my aunt's?"

As she spoke, her eyes met her brother's, and she knew that like her, he wanted to laugh.

Instead, she walked into the house while he got into the Chaise and drove away.

There was no sign of Atkins, and the Porter said kindly:

"You'll find Sir Trevor's rooms on the Second Floor, Miss."

"Thank you," Angela replied, and started up the stair.

They were steep and got steeper after she had passed the First Floor.

She reached a small landing with two doors, one of which was open. She could see it was the bedroom.

The other, she guessed, was the Sitting-Room.

Atkins put her trunk down in the bedroom and opened the door of the Sitting-Room for her.

It was well furnished, she thought, if in rather dull colours.

As it was at the end of the street, there was a bow window looking out onto another street which crossed the end of it.

There seemed to be a lot of traffic and a number of people walking about.

She enjoyed looking out on a different view from the one she was used to at home.

There she had the gardens, the trees, and a distant view over the Estate.

Atkins came into the room.

"Would ye like a cup o' tea, Miss," he asked, "or somethin' stronger?"

"I would love a cup of tea," Angela answered.

She realised that while he was speaking he was staring at her.

Then he said:

"If I 'adn't seen it wiv' me own eyes, I wouldn't 'ave believed it!"

"Believed—what?" Angela asked.

"That anyone could look like an Angel an' it not be due to paint an' powder, so t' speak."

Angela laughed.

"No, it is quite natural, and I can assure you, I put nothing on my face."

"I c'n see that, Miss," Atkins said, "an' very pretty ye are too, if ye don't mind me sayin' so!"

"No—I am flattered," Angela murmured.

She thought it was a strange conversation to be having with a servant.

When Trevor joined her, she said in a whisper:

"Did you tell your valet that you were going to bring back somebody who looked like an Angel?"

"I did not tell him," Trevor replied, "but I told a friend of mine, somewhat indiscreetly, I admit, that I was going to the country to find an Angel for George Edwardes, and he must have been listening at the door."

"He does not know I am your sister?" Angela whispered.

"No, of course not," Trevor answered. "For God's sake, Angela, be careful! Although I trust Atkins and he is very loyal, all servants talk, as you know."

Angela wanted to say that Higgins had no-one to talk to, but she thought it was beside the point.

It was foolish of Trevor, if he wanted to keep everything quiet, she thought, to have told one of his friends that he was going to find an Angel.

As if he knew what she was thinking, Trevor said:

"What I really said to my friend was that I had a *Chère Amie* who looked like an Angel."

Angela thought everything seemed to be growing more and more complicated.

She drank the tea that Atkins had brought her, while Trevor had a glass of brandy.

She was surprised he was drinking so early in the day.

She looked at the glass in his hand and, as if she had asked the question, he said:

"I need something to steady my nerves. We must both be careful, for as you know, one slip and there would be no going back."

"Stop frightening me!" Angela said. "What are we going to do now?"

She thought they must be going somewhere because Trevor had not suggested she should take off her hat.

He glanced at the clock on the mantelpiece.

"We are going to the Gaiety Theatre," he said. "George Edwardes will be there in another quarter-of-an-hour."

Angela gave a little cry.

"But, surely, I ought to try and look smart before I meet him?"

"What you are wearing will make him realise

that he has to provide you with everything—and I mean everything!" Trevor said. "Come along, we will take a Hansom Cab."

He went from the room to tell Atkins to find one.

When Angela walked down the stairs, it was already at the door.

She had never been in a Hansom Cab before.

She found it very exciting to be sitting beside Trevor with the door folded across them.

The Cabman climbed up behind.

They drove off, and Angela thought it seemed a little insecure, but very thrilling.

She put her hand into her brother's.

"I was thinking when we were driving up to London that this was an adventure," she said, "but I can see that for me it is going to be a series of adventures. I love driving like this."

"You are being a good sport," Trevor said, "but do not forget that we have to be very affectionate towards one another."

He paused, and then continued:

"It would be a great mistake when we arrive at the Marquis's if other men think they can step in and push me out."

Angela looked at him in surprise.

"Why should they want to do that?" she asked.

Trevor parted his lips to tell her, then thought it would be a mistake.

He was astute enough to realise that what was so original and unique about his sister, besides her looks, was that she was so innocent.

She was unaware of anything that went on in the world in which he moved.

The Hansom Cab did not take long moving down Piccadilly and through the Circus to the Gaiety.

It looked, Angela thought, a little drab.

Then she remembered that it would be lit up at night and that, she thought, would make all the difference.

Trevor paid off the Cabby.

He took her across the pavement and down a narrow side alley to where written, so that there could be no mistake, were the words:

STAGE DOOR

It was early and there were only three people waiting outside it.

Trevor knew that later there would be a whole crowd.

They would be waiting to see the Gaiety Girls they knew or recognised, and of course the Principals of the Show.

He walked quickly through the narrow door.

Just inside there was a window and a man sitting behind it.

" 'Evenin', Sir Trevor!" the man said before he could speak. "You're early t'night."

"I need to see Mr. Edwardes before he gets too busy," Trevor answered.

The Porter made a gesture as if to say that was impossible.

"Tell him," Trevor said, "I have brought somebody he particularly wanted to see and it is important that he should meet her alone."

The Porter, who was a great personality at the Gaiety Theatre, glanced casually at Angela.

Then he stiffened.

Trevor, watching him, saw his eyes widen and his jaw drop in astonishment.

Then he said:

"Leave it t'me, Sir Trevor. I'll not be long."

He hurried away, and Trevor drew Angela farther inside.

There was an iron staircase leading up to the next floor and corridors going in both directions.

To Angela's surprise, it looked very unglamorous and, she thought, rather dirty.

Just under the stairs there was a large bin to hold waste paper or anything else that was unwanted.

But those who used it had been casual enough to throw a lot of what should have gone into the bin onto the floor.

There appeared to be nobody to pick up the old programmes, pieces of paper, an empty cigar-box, as well as some empty bottles.

Trevor had moved Angela back against a wall.

People were passing, hurrying in one direction or another.

There were page-boys and men carrying what appeared to be props for the stage.

As they waited, a few women came in through the Stage-Door.

They hurried up the stairs, or down the corridor.

They did not look glamorous or prepossessing, and they were certainly not beautiful, as the Gaiety Girls were reputed to be.

As if he knew what Angela was thinking, Trevor said:

"They are the Dressers."

Angela felt somehow relieved.

It was bad enough to see the inside of the Theatre.

She did not also want the disillusionment of finding that the Gaiety Girls, about whom she had heard so much, were very different off stage from what they were on stage.

The Porter came back.

"Mr. Edwardes'll see you, Sir Trevor," he said, " 'e's in 'is office. I'll see that no-one disturbs ye."

"Thank you," Trevor said.

He pressed something into the Porter's hand, and Angela saw just the flicker of gold.

She thought, if it was half a sovereign, let alone a whole one, it was more than they could afford.

Trevor was walking quickly ahead of her, and she followed him.

He opened a door which she thought was not far from the stage.

She found herself in a small office in which there was a large desk and three hard chairs.

The walls were completely covered with posters advertising the Shows that George Edwardes had put on at the Gaiety.

There were quite a number of them, and she noticed that all the titles carried the word "Girl" in them.

She could see on the posters the names "The Stage Girl," "My Girl," "The Circus Girl," "The Runaway Girl."

She remembered reading somewhere that the first of these, "The Gaiety Girl," had been such a success and had run for so many months that George Edwardes had made the word his talisman and was afraid not to use it.

On the desk there were piles of press-cuttings besides a number of newspapers.

She guessed these all referred to the present Show, which was called "Cinder-Ellen Up-to-Date."

Then she looked at George Edwardes himself.

He was a red-faced, cheerful-looking man, not as tall or as overwhelming as she had expected him to be.

Her brother was shaking his hand.

"How are you, George?" he asked. "I have brought you what I promised, and I do not think you will be disappointed."

"I hope not, Sir Trevor," George Edwardes replied, "because I am desperate. I have looked everywhere, everywhere I can think of, and there is nobody who is suitable to take Lucy's place."

"Then let me introduce you to Angela!" Trevor said.

He looked towards his sister as he spoke and put out his hand to draw her forward.

She had been behind him so that George Edwardes had not noticed her until that moment.

She saw his eyes taking in her appearance, at first casually, as if he thought it was unlikely she would be what he wanted.

Then his expression changed and became one of surprise coupled with an excitement he could not suppress.

"I don't believe it!" he said beneath his breath.

Then sharply, giving an order, he said:

"Take off your hat!"

Angela obeyed him, pulling out the hat-pins which had kept her hat in place while they were driving.

She pushed her golden curls into place.

"Where the devil did you find anyone like this?" George Edwardes asked in a low voice.

"I have known her for years," Trevor replied lightly. "She lives not far from my house in the country."

George Edwardes walked towards Angela.

He moved round her as if he must take her in from every angle and perhaps in doing so find a flaw.

Then he gave a deep sigh.

"All I can say, Sir Trevor," he said, "is that you have solved my problem and I don't know how to thank you."

"I shall be quite content with the thousand pounds you promised me," Trevor said, "and, of course, you realise that as Angela comes from the country, she has little to wear except what she has on."

George Edwardes made a sweeping gesture with his hand.

"That is immaterial," he said. "I want to hear her speak."

He stood in front of Angela and said:

"Now, tell me your name and if you are prepared to play the part of an Angel."

"My name is Angela," Angela replied.

As she spoke, she remembered that Trevor had

not told her what other name she should have.

Quickly, before she could say any more, her brother chipped in:

"Angela is what she was christened and, as far as you are concerned, George, that is all you need to know."

He paused, and then continued:

"There might be trouble with her family if it was learned that she was going on the stage, so to speak."

George Edwardes laughed.

" 'So to speak' is right! His Lordship's stage is somewhat different from mine."

"I know, but there is no point in Angels being anything but anonymous," Trevor remarked.

George Edwardes laughed.

"Very well. 'Angela' it shall be, but I want to hear more."

"What do you want me to say," Angela asked, "except that I am finding it very exciting to be here, and, of course, I have heard from . . . S-sir Trevor how famous you are."

She just stumbled slightly over her brother's title.

She thought, however, that George Edwardes would put it down to shyness.

"Perfect!" George Edwardes exclaimed. "All I can say, Sir Trevor, is that if you want a job, you can come and help me cast my next Show if you can find winners like this one!"

"I am keeping my fingers crossed that she will satisfy the Marquis," Trevor said.

"She'll 'knock spots' off Lucy, and if he is not satisfied, I'll eat my hat!" George Edwardes replied.

"Now, what about clothes?" Trevor asked, wishing to 'get down to brass tacks.'

"Nelly'll have to see to that," George Edwardes replied.

He moved from his desk and banged his hand down on a bell.

It rang and seemed at the same time to echo round the small room.

The door was opened almost immediately by a page-boy.

"Fetch Nelly to me," George Edwardes commanded, "and be quick about it."

"Very good, Mr. Edwardes," the page-boy replied.

"Now, suppose you sit down, Angela," George Edwardes said, "and you, too, Sir Trevor. I think we should have a drink to celebrate this. It has taken a load off my mind which kept me awake last night, I can tell you that!"

He did not wait for an answer, but went to a cupboard at the side of the room.

When he opened it, Angela could see rows and rows of bottles and glasses inside it.

"Now, what do Angels drink?" he asked.

"I think champagne would be appropriate," Trevor replied.

"I'm much obliged to you," George Edwardes answered, "you have done me a good turn, and no mistake. I was dreading having to tell 'His Nibs' that Lucy was still *hors de combat*."

"Is she still bad?" Trevor asked.

"I enquired at Luncheon time," George Edwardes replied, "and her temperature was one hundred three degrees! If you ask me, she'll be out of the Show for at least a week!"

"I suppose it is that fever that has been going around," Trevor remarked.

Because Angela knew him so well, she knew he was delighted that there was no chance of Lucy returning unexpectedly.

He would therefore not lose the money George Edwardes had promised him.

A bottle of champagne was produced, and George Edwardes poured out three glasses.

"We'll drink a toast," he said. "May the Angel you brought me bring us all the blessings we require, including a big cheque from the Marquis for my next production!"

When he had finished speaking, he poured all the champagne in his glass down his throat.

"I will drink to that, and so will Angela," Trevor replied, "but you are not to frighten her. She is very, very afraid of failing us."

"She'll fail no-one with a face like that!" George Edwardes replied.

He looked towards Angela and said:

"If you want a job with me after this weekend, I promise I'll seriously consider it."

"Thank you," Angela replied. "I can only pray that I shall not fail either of you."

She glanced at Trevor as she spoke, thinking how much it meant to him.

To her surprise, he took hold of her hand which was not holding the glass and raised it to his lips.

"You have not failed me," he said in a voice he had never used to her before.

For a moment she was surprised.

Then she realised he was playing the part of what she had called a *cher ami*.

She therefore smiled at him and knew as she did so that George Edwardes was watching them.

There was a knock on the door, and without waiting to be told to enter a woman came in.

She was middle-aged, rather haggard-looking, with a great many lines on her face, and her hair had turned grey.

"Here you are, Nelly!" George Edwardes said. "I've got a big job for you, and I want it done, needless to say, in double-quick time."

"An' what is it you're asking, Mr. Edwardes?" Nelly asked sharply. "You knows as well as I do that I'm up to me eyes, an' Heaven knows what you'll think o' the girl as is takin' Lucy's part!"

"What happens to-night is immaterial," George Edwardes replied. "Let me introduce you to the Angel who is taking Lucy's part in His Lordship's Play."

He made a gesture with his hand towards Angela.

Nelly, who had not noticed her before, turned to look at her.

For a moment she was silent. Then she said:

"As Heaven's my judge, I can only believe me eyes are deceiving me!"

George Edwardes laughed.

"That is what I thought, and we can thank Sir Trevor for finding her."

"Well, all I can say is he's a Magician or a Witch-Doctor if ever there was one!"

Trevor smiled.

"That is exactly what I like to hear from you, Nelly," he said, "and now you have to make Angela look the part."

"I don't have to do nothing to 'er face," Nelly said, "but her clothes . . . ! Where on earth can she 'ave got them from?"

Angela laughed.

"I am afraid they are from the country and very old."

"They certainly look like it!" Nelly replied. "Oh, well, come along with me and we'll see what we can do with you."

Angela looked a little uncertainly at her brother.

"Go with Nelly," he said, "and keep out of sight of everybody."

He turned to Nelly.

"You do understand," he said, "that it would be a great mistake for Angela to be seen by anybody before she arrives at Vaux?"

"You don't have to tell me," Nelly said. "If them rats with their top-hats get so much of a glimpse at her, they'll be after her like flying hawks, as you well knows."

The two men laughed at Nelly's expressions which actually were famous in the Theatre.

"Sir Trevor's right," George Edwardes said, "but keep her out of sight and lock the door."

"When you have dressed her," Trevor said, "I will take her away and give her some dinner. We will meet the rest of the Gang when we join the Marquis's private railway carriage at the Station."

"You have certainly got a surprise for him!" George Edwardes said.

Nelly hustled Angela out of the office, saying:

"Put yer 'at on and pull it down over your face. As the Gentleman said, it'd be a mistake for anyone to see you afore His Lordship does."

They went to the end of the corridor, where Nelly opened a door into a room which was very large.

It was the most fantastic room Angela had ever seen.

There were gowns hanging from ropes which crossed it and ran up as high as the ceiling.

There were, in fact, three lines of gowns.

Then there were cupboards on either side of the room, the doors of which were open.

Each cupboard contained more gowns hanging on hangers.

They filled them completely.

The shelves above them contained hats.

Never had Angela imagined such a kaleidoscope of colour and a profusion of feathers, flowers, and glittering diamanté.

She stood gasping at what she saw.

Then she was aware that Nelly was shouting for her assistants.

There were three of them, and they came running.

One was young, but the other two were older women who had obviously worked with Nelly for years.

She began giving them orders for underclothes and silk stockings. She asked the size of Angela's feet.

Before she could realise what was happening, Angela found herself half-naked while the assistants were putting various items on the table.

Never had she imagined that anything could be as beautiful as the underclothes which she was told every Gaiety Girl wore.

They were of pure silk, appliquéd with real lace.

The stockings were also silk from the tops to the toes.

Angela thought nervously that they looked very delicate.

Nelly's assistants found her shoes which fitted her exactly.

They had high heels and were very much more elegant than anything she had ever owned.

Then there was a pause when Nelly described the clothes she should wear:

"She's an Angel, an' Angels wear white. Come on, girls, let me have everything white an' we'll see what fits her."

Strangely enough, when everything seemed to be so colourful, there was a considerable number of white gowns.

It was very different from what Angela had expected in the Theatre.

Some were of chiffon, which were very delicate.

They made her look slim, as if she might float away.

One was of lace and so delicate that she was afraid Nelly would say she could not have it.

Several gowns were embellished with embroidery or had patches of colour on them.

They were sent away immediately.

Finally Angela was supplied with enough gowns, she thought, to last her for years.

But Nelly seemed to think she needed them for the two days she was staying at Vaux.

Then one of the assistants asked:

"What about a ridin'-habit? Yer knows th' Marquis 'as a lot of 'orses an' she'll be expected to ride them."

Angela, who had said very little, gave an exclamation of excitement.

"Do you really think I will be able to ride while I am staying with the Marquis?"

"I'll be very surprised if you don't," Nelly exclaimed. "That's if you want to. We've heard enough about 'is 'orses! There's not a soul in the Gaiety as 'adn't made a bob or two when 'e's racin' them!"

"How wonderful!" Angela exclaimed. "Oh, please, do find me a habit! The one I have at home is threadbare!"

"That's not somethin' you can take to Vaux!" Nelly said sharply.

One of the women had already run off to find what she required.

She brought back two habits.

One was of very pale blue that was almost the colour of Angela's eyes.

"It is lovely, but I could not wear that!" she exclaimed. "I am sure people would be shocked if my habit was not black or navy-blue."

"Those be colours for them as calls themselves 'Ladies,'" Nelly said sarcastically. "When you leaves 'ere, you're one of the Gaiety Girls wearing clothes as belongs to the Gaiety. This one 'ad a great success when Nelly Taylor wore it."

Angela realised she had made a mistake and had been thinking of herself as a "Lady" instead of an actress.

"Then I would love to wear it," she said quietly. "Thank you very much!"

There was another habit very much the same, only in pale leaf green.

"Put them both in," Nelly said. "You can't be seen twice in the same outfit!"

Angela thought of how long she had worn her own clothes and gave a little laugh.

"Now, don't laugh, young lady," Nelly said. "You may be an Angel in your own right, but you're representin' us. At the Gaiety we've got our reputation to keep us, haven't we, Girls?"

There was a chorus of: "Course we 'ave!" and Nelly went on:

"If you don't knock 'em 'ead over-'eels when you appears in them evening-gowns, then I'll give up me job an' retire!"

The other helpers laughed.

"You knows we couldn't do wi'out you, Nelly!"

"That's true," Nelly said complacently. "An' I'm not askin' for any criticism where Angels is concerned."

"Of course not, and there will not be any," Angela said. "Thank you very, very much. I am very grateful. I never imagined that I would wear such beautiful, exciting clothes! I hope I will be able to tell you afterwards what everybody said about them."

"I'll be waitin'," Nelly said. "Now, pack everything up, Girls, I am going to take our Angel back to Mr. Edwardes."

She went to the door and unlocked it.

She peeped out and quickly locked the door again.

"Now, look here," she said to Angela, "they said you was not to be seen 'til you boards the train after the Show. The place out there is already full to bursting!"

"Then what am I to do?" Angela asked.

Nelly looked towards a hat on top of the wardrobe.

She got it down and brought it back to Angela.

"Now, put this on," she said, "and pull the veil down well over your face."

While Nelly had been reaching for the hat, Angela had been putting on the dress in which she had come.

Nelly, suddenly aware of what she was doing, gave a screech of horror.

"You're not goin' out in them rags!" she said. "What am I thinkin' of? I must be losin' me mind!"

She looked at the others as if it were their fault.

"A travelling-gown!" she said. "Somethin' very attractive, but not white. Young, very young!"

They ran as quickly as they could and came back with two outfits at which Nelly looked in disdain.

Angela thought they were the most attractive things she had ever seen.

One was of silk with a skirt that touched the ground and had two rows of frills round the bottom of it.

The fitted coatee ended at the waist and was encircled by a sash.

It was of the same blue which Nelly had chosen for her riding-habit.

When she put it on she knew that never in her whole life had she looked smarter or appeared to have such an elegant figure.

Nelly then took away the hat she had chosen for her to wear and discovered another one.

It was worn on the back of the head so that it made a halo for Angela's golden curls.

Nelly looked at her critically.

"There's somethin' missin'," she said.

"I cannot believe it is anything but perfect!" Angela cried.

Nelly put up her hands.

"No, you're looking like a Society girl, not what you should be—a Gaiety Girl!"

Nelly gave sharp orders to her assistants.

A mirror was put on the table in front of Angela together with some pots and tubes which she knew were cosmetics.

"You can say that you don't need this," Nelly said, "but I'm going to give you a touch of rouge on your cheeks and some salve on your lips. Your eyes is exactly right as they are."

"I've never seen anyone wiv such long eye-lashes!" one of the helpers exclaimed.

"That's wot I was thinkin'," Nelly answered, "an' an Angel wouldn't look right if they wore mascara."

They laughed at this.

Nelly powdered Angela's face very lightly.

She then stood back to inspect her handiwork.

"Now, don't go an' overdo it," she said. "Everyone when they starts puts on too much, an' if you asks me, the Almighty knows best!"

" 'Specially when it comes to Angels!" someone quipped sharply. "An' if 'Is Lordship ain't bowled over by 'er, then all I can say is—he must be blind!"

Angela saw one of the helpers nudge the other as if at a secret joke.

It made her feel apprehensive.

Perhaps, however, much as Nelly had tried to make her look the part, the Marquis would find fault.

Then she was sure that by this time George Edwardes would have given Trevor the thousand pounds he had promised him.

She sent up a little prayer that there would not be a hitch.

Then Nelly said:

"Here's a handbag with all your needs in it. Now, come on, move fast an' keep your head down."

Angela rose to her feet, and Nelly unlocked the door.

There was the sound of chattering voices and people moving about.

"Follow me!" Nelly ordered.

She hurried forward, literally pushing people out of her way as she said:

"Come on, come on! The curtain'll be goin' up an' you'll be late if you don't 'urry!"

One of the girls in the passage gave a little scream and ran up the stairs.

If anybody glanced at Angela as she hurried after

Nelly, she was not aware of it.

She had her head down, and she reached the office without there being any interruptions.

Nelly paused and waited for her to reach her side.

Then she flung open the door and shouted:

"Hey, presto! The curtain rises!"

chapter three

As they drove away from the Gaiety Theatre, again in a Hansom Cab, Trevor said:

"Well, you have taken the first fence in style!"

"Do I really look all right?" Angela asked.

"You know perfectly well you look smashing!" he replied. "And George Edwardes was going into ecstasies about you."

"I was very nervous that he would be critical," Angela replied.

"Nobody is going to be critical where you are concerned," Trevor said, "and remember, I am your *cher ami* and you are very fond of me."

"That is true, at any rate," Angela replied, "but I am terrified of all these lies. As Nanny always used to say, 'One lie leads to another'!"

Trevor laughed.

"I remember her saying that, and spanking me because I lied to her."

Angela was not really listening.

She was looking out at the streets through which they were passing.

When they had gone a little way, she realised they had narrowed and were darker.

"Where are we going?" she asked.

"I am taking you to dine at a small place where nobody will see us," he answered. "Then, after I have collected my clothes, we will go back to the Theatre and pick up your boxes before we take the train to Vaux."

Angela thought it was rather frustrating, but there was no point in saying so.

Also, the apprehension she felt about meeting the Marquis was growing with everything she heard about him.

It seemed extraordinary that George Edwardes, who was so successful and had made the Gaiety Girls the talk of London, should be nervous of anyone.

As if again he guessed what she was thinking, Trevor said:

"By the way, George Edwardes gave me the cheque and I have it in my pocket."

"Oh, Trevor, how wonderful! You will put it in the Bank at once?"

"I promise I will do that as soon as I can," Trevor answered.

"It will help us for the moment," Angela murmured, "but what of the future? Have you received any more commissions?"

"If I had, I would have told you about them," Trevor replied.

He spoke sharply.

She felt it was a sore point and it would be best not to mention it again.

The Hansom Cab came to a stop outside what looked like a small Restaurant in a badly-lit street.

Angela stepped out.

As she entered the Restaurant, she was aware that everybody turned to look at her in her smart new clothes.

The Proprietor obviously knew Trevor and welcomed him effusively.

He showed them to what appeared to be the best table.

The Restaurant was very small, but furnished, although Angela was not aware of it, like a French *Bistro*.

The Proprietor and Trevor consulted the menu which was written in longhand and talked about the food for some time.

Having decided what they should eat, the Proprietor went through a door which Angela thought led to the Kitchen.

Then a young waiter brought them a bottle of champagne.

Angela looked at it critically.

"Are we not being rather extravagant?" she asked.

"I feel we have cause to celebrate what is in my pocket," Trevor said.

The wine-waiter poured out the champagne and Trevor raised his glass.

"To an Angel," he said, "who really is raining blessings from Heaven upon a mere mortal."

"Do not speak too quickly!" Angela begged.

They had to wait for quite a time before the food appeared.

As soon as she tasted the first dish, Angela knew that it was delicious.

Also it was different from anything she had ever eaten before.

Trevor was watching her.

"Before you ask me," he said, "the Chef is French. I discovered this place about a month ago and have sent a number of people here."

"There are not many here at the moment," Angela remarked.

She looked round the small Restaurant as she spoke and saw there were only three other couples besides themselves.

"It is early yet," Trevor answered. "People dine later in London than they do in the country."

They were finishing their second course, when a smartly dressed man accompanied by a woman, who looked to Angela very exotic, came in.

The Proprietor took them to a table.

The Gentleman was just about to sit down, when he saw Trevor.

"Hello, old boy!" he said, walking up to him. "I called round to your place this morning, but they said you had gone to the country."

"And so I had," Trevor replied, "but, as you see, I have returned."

The man who was speaking to him was looking at Angela.

Somewhat reluctantly Trevor said:

"This, my dear, is an old friend of mine—Lord Grentham."

Angela held out her hand.

"Surely anyone as beautiful as you must have a name?" Lord Grentham remarked.

"Her name is Angela," Trevor said, again reluctantly.

"Is that all?"

"That is quite enough, as far as you are concerned," Trevor replied, "and I think the Lady you brought with you is growing impatient."

Lord Grentham's eyes twinkled.

"You are making it very clear that you have no wish for my company, but I am sure I can contrive somehow to meet Angela again."

He smiled at her as he spoke.

Then, as Trevor said nothing, he moved to where the Lady he had brought with him was sitting.

When he was out of hearing, Angela said:

"You were rather disagreeable to him."

"He is someone I have no wish for you to know," Trevor replied.

"But you said he is an old friend of yours."

"I have a great many friends who are not suitable to be yours," Trevor replied, "and George is one of them. He is a *Roué*, and nice girls run away when they see him coming."

Angela laughed.

"You forget I am not a 'Nice Girl' at the moment, but, to all intents and purposes, a Gaiety Girl."

Trevor held up his hands.

"God forbid you should ever be that!"

"But, why, when you all say how beautiful they are and every man in London wants to see them and take them out to supper."

Trevor did not answer.

He looked at his watch.

"I think we should be going," he said. "You have a great deal to do before we catch the train, and it would be a mistake to miss it!"

Angela did not say anything.

She thought, however, that the reason her brother was in such a hurry to leave the Restaurant was because of Lord Grentham.

She looked at him without appearing to do so and thought he looked very raffish.

At the same time, he was attractive.

He was obviously having an altercation with the woman with him.

Only as Trevor paid the bill and rose did he realise they were leaving.

He hurried across the Restaurant as they walked to the door.

"Leaving so early, old boy?" he asked Trevor. "Shall I see you at the Gaiety after the Show?"

"No, I will not be there to-night," Trevor replied. "As a matter of fact, I am staying with Vauxhall and hope to have a chance of riding his horses."

Lord Grentham looked surprised and said:

"Is the Marquis having a party? Why has he not asked me?"

He was speaking to Trevor, but he was looking at Angela.

Trevor pushed open the door.

"I will see you next week, George," he said. "I expect we will be attending the same parties."

If Lord Grentham replied, Angela did not hear him.

She felt her brother pushing her out of the Restaurant.

Obediently she walked out onto the pavement.

Trevor joined her and hailed an empty Hansom Cab which was passing by.

As they drove off, he said:

"I had no idea that Grentham would turn up to-night. It was a mistake to tell him about the place, and a good deed never goes unpunished."

"Why are you so against him?" Angela asked.

"Because he is the sort of man Mama would not like you to know. He is, however, very influential and I have no wish to pick a quarrel with him."

"And you think you might quarrel with him over me?" Angela asked.

"I saw the way he was looking at you," Trevor said angrily. "I would not trust him with any woman, let alone my sister!"

Angela thought it was nice of her brother to be so protective.

She put her hand on his arm and said:

"Do not worry about me, Trevor. You know as well as I do that when I have played the part of the Angel for the Marquis, I shall disappear, never to be seen again."

She paused, and then continued:

"In any case, I certainly could not afford to stay in London."

She thought Trevor looked slightly relieved, and went on:

"Also, do not forget that I shall look very different when these clothes go back to the Gaiety. Nelly made it very clear that they were on loan to me."

"I know that," Trevor replied, "and for God's sake do not spoil them. There was a fearful row last week when one of the Girls spilt a cup of coffee on her gown and it had to be replaced."

"Does George Edwardes supply all the Girls with their clothes?" Angela asked.

"Most of them," Trevor replied. "They are the best advertisement he could possibly have for his Shows. When the Girls appear at Romano's or any of the other smart places for supper, everybody stares at them as if they were still behind the foot-lights!"

Angela thought this must be exciting, but she said a little wistfully:

"I suppose there is no chance of my seeing them on the stage to-night?"

Trevor thought for a moment.

"I tell you what we will do," he said. "Because you have been so kind as to help me, I will see if there is a place in the box that George Edwardes always uses himself."

He paused and then said:

"We can slip in there for a short while before we collect your clothes from Nelly. Then we will go straight to the Station."

Angela clasped her hands together.

"Can we really do that? Oh, thank you, thank you, Trevor. I know it will be thrilling!"

"You must understand that you are not to talk to anybody," Trevor warned. "If anyone tries to talk to you, just ignore them or else walk away."

He paused before he said:

"I suppose really you ought to stay in the carriage and wait while I go into the Theatre alone."

"Oh, please, Trevor, please!" Angela said. "If I can just have a glimpse of the stage and the Gaiety Girls on it, I shall understand better what it is all about and how I should look when I play the part the Marquis requires me to."

"Very well," Trevor said, "but only if you do exactly as I say. If there is any trouble, I shall be very angry."

Angela could not imagine what trouble there could be.

She was delighted at the idea of seeing the actual stage of the Gaiety.

She thought it would be a mistake to go on talking about it in case Trevor changed his mind.

They reached his Lodgings in Half Moon Street to find that Atkins had packed Trevor's clothes in two trunks.

"You seem to be taking a lot of luggage for just two days in the country!" Angela remarked.

"It is my riding-boots that take up so much of the room," her brother replied.

"Nelly gave me two very spectacular riding-habits," Angela said. "Do you think I shall be allowed to ride?"

"Of course you will," Trevor replied, "and if you are not a good actress, you are certainly a very good rider, and that it something the Marquis will appreciate."

Angela raised her face and kissed her brother's cheek.

"This adventure is really getting exciting," she said. "Thank you, Trevor, for suggesting it."

"I only hope you will feel the same when it is all over," Trevor said. "Now, come along, if you are going to see the last part of the Show."

There was no sign of Atkins, so Trevor carried his trunks down the stairs.

The Porter, who was a different one from the one who had been on duty during the day, hailed him a Hansom Cab.

Trevor's trunks were attached to it with ropes and they drove off to the Gaiety Theatre.

The crowd outside the Stage-Door was enormous.

One or two of the women seemed to recognise Trevor.

They all stared curiously at Angela.

Because she was shy, she almost ran through the Stage-Door.

She could hear the music coming from the Orchestra.

Just as she and Trevor entered, a crowd of Girls whose costumes consisted mostly of feathers came hurrying off the stage.

They ran up the stairs and, seeing Trevor, one of them shouted:

"Hallo, Baronet! We missed you in your usual seat."

Angela looked at Trevor enquiringly.

"Do you come here every night?" she asked.

"I come here a great deal," he answered quickly, "because I meet the people who are likely to require horses, houses, and anything else I can find for them."

He did not meet her eyes as he spoke.

She was sure there were other reasons as well.

Trevor spoke to one of the men who seemed to be in charge of what was going on.

Angela could not hear what he said.

Then he turned back and took her by the arm to lead her down the corridor.

She had a quick glimpse of somebody on the stage.

At the side of the stage, girls in very elaborate costumes were waiting to go on.

It was only a quick glimpse.

Then Angela heard a man singing in a deep baritone.

Trevor led her on without speaking.

He opened the door of the stage box where there were three people; one of them was George Edwardes.

Without speaking, he indicated to Angela a seat at the back of the box behind the others.

She could see the stage perfectly.

The man singing was wearing evening clothes, with a top-hat and carrying a cane.

His song was vaguely familiar to her.

She had no idea that it was one that had swept London and was whistled by the errand-boys.

She thought only that it was tuneful and the singer had a delightful voice.

Then she realised that Trevor had left her and thought he had gone to find Nelly and collect her clothes.

The singer went off amid a roar of applause.

He took half-a-dozen calls before the lights went down.

Then, almost immediately, the curtain rose.

Although Angela knew very little about the Theatre, she guessed this was the Grande Finale.

There was a flight of stairs at the back of the stage.

Grouped around it were the Chorus Girls, all wearing gowns which glittered and glimmmered in the lights.

It was certainly very spectacular.

Then down the staircase came the stars, one by one.

Each in turn received a great roar of applause.

Then the Gaiety Girls came down three at a time, all exquisitely dressed.

The whole Theatre clapped and shouted until it was impossible to hear the Orchestra.

Then bouquets were carried onto the stage and a great many were flung from the audience.

It was something Angela had never imagined.

The enthusiasm and excitement seemed to affect the performers as much as those who watched them.

They curtsied, smiled, bowed, and waved.

At last the Orchestra struck up the National Anthem.

Everybody sang "God Save the Queen" with gusto, which Angela found very moving.

She felt the tears come into her eyes.

Then the door of the box opened and Trevor came to her side.

He did not speak, he merely took her hand and pulled her to her feet.

She wanted to ask if she could stay a little longer and see what would happen next.

But he pulled her out into the passage and closed the door.

"Hurry," he said, "and keep your head down. I do not want to be delayed by the 'Stage-Door Johnnies.' "

Angela did not know what he meant.

Suddenly she saw, standing just inside the door where the Porter's box was, at least a dozen young men.

They were wearing evening clothes and carrying top-hats and canes.

In fact, they were just like the man who had been on the stage singing.

Briskly Trevor moved through them, pushing them aside in his effort to make way for Angela.

One of the men was about to expostulate with him.

Then he saw Angela and stared in amazement as he swept off his hat.

"Good-evening, beautiful Lady!" he said.

Angela, however, had no chance of answering.

Trevor had her tightly by the arm.

He pulled her out through the door, fighting his way through the crowd to where the carriage was waiting.

He helped Angela into it and told the Cabby to drive to Paddington Station.

As they drove away from the Theatre, Trevor gave a sigh of relief.

"I hope you are satisfied," he said.

"Oh, thank you, thank you, Trevor!" Angela answered. "It was wonderful! I only wish I could have seen more."

" 'Enough is as good as a feast'!" Trevor remarked. "And I have no wish for you to be ogled by all those hang-abouts."

"They looked very smart," Angela said. "I suppose they can afford to give big parties at Romano's and the other places you have talked about."

"They can afford it, right enough," Trevor said bitterly, "while I have to wait for invitations, as I am unable to pay for myself."

Angela slipped her arm through his.

"I know it is difficult, Dearest," she said, "but now we do have some money to repair the Priory, and you remember how happy Papa and Mama were there."

"They did not have to worry about money," Trevor argued. "They could afford to have decent horses and, you remember, we used to have a Shoot in those days."

"Yes, I know," Angela replied, "but I feel it will all happen again, and we just need to have a little patience."

"That is the only thing that does not cost any money!" Trevor said.

Angela gave a cry.

"What about the cheque? You did say you would send it to the Bank."

"I did not forget," Trevor answered, "and I have put it on my dressing-table with instructions for Atkins to post it first thing to-morrow morning."

Angela gave a cry of relief.

"That was good of you. I was so afraid you might lose it or something."

"I am not as foolish as that," Trevor answered, "and I suggest you make the most of your visit to the Marquis's house, because it is somewhere you will never go again."

"Supposing, just supposing," Angela murmured, "the Marquis should invite me for a second time?"

Trevor sat upright.

"Now, listen, Angela," he said. "You are doing this so that we can save the Priory from becoming any more dilapidated than it is at the moment. But you must realise that it is something of which Mama would have violently disapproved, and so would all our relatives."

He went on more forcefully:

"The moment your part is finished, you must disappear as if you had never existed, or had gone back to Heaven! No-one, and I mean no-one, who is at the Marquis's house, must ever hear of you again."

Trevor spoke so positively that Angela knew he meant every word of it.

She did not answer because she was thinking it really would be a question of a "Cinderella."

Her beautiful clothes would disappear at midnight and she would be left in only her rags.

"We should not be doing this," Trevor went on when she did not speak. "It is worrying me to death when I see the effect you have on people like Grentham, and I shall be on tenterhooks the whole time we are at Vaux."

"Do not worry," Angela said. "I feel, perhaps because we are both so desperate, that Papa and Mama are helping us by thinking up ways by which we can make some money. All the same, it is a very exciting adventure for me!"

She looked up at her brother and pleaded:

"Please, do not spoil it, for even if I have to go back to the country and never again come to London, it will be something to remember."

She paused, and then continued:

"In fact, I shall never forget my glimpse of the Gaiety and how beautiful the Gaiety Girls looked as they walked down the stairs."

Unexpectedly Trevor bent and kissed his sister on the cheek.

"Poor little Angela!" he said. "You are very sensible and very brave, and I am very proud of you. It may be hard, but we will win this race if it is the last thing we do!"

"Of course we will," Angela said confidently, "and when we look back on it, we will think how clever we have been!"

The nearer they got to Paddington Station, the more Angela was aware of how nervous her brother was.

They got out of the Cab, and Angela saw for the first time the luggage which Trevor had collected for her from the Gaiety.

There were three large trunks of it and what she had not expected, two hat-boxes.

It required two Porters to transport it from the Hackney Carriage.

The Marquis's private coach was waiting, attached to a train at a side platform.

Angela had never seen a private coach before, but she was most impressed by its appearance.

It was painted red and white and looked, she thought, somewhat theatrical, with the Marquis's crest on the doors.

There were Stewards wearing the Marquis's livery who welcomed Trevor.

"Good-evenin', Sir Trevor!" one of them said. "You're early, but everythin's in readiness."

"There is rather a lot of luggage," Trevor replied. "Are we the first?"

"Yes, Sir Trevor, but I 'spect the rest of 'Is Lordship's guests'll be arrivin' within the next fifteen minutes."

Trevor escorted Angela to the train.

She was thrilled by what was known as the "Drawing-Room."

It was furnished with sofas and armchairs covered in red damask.

There were pictures on the walls and curtains at the windows.

Because she was obviously so interested, one of the Stewards showed her the small Kitchen and Pantry.

There was also a bedroom with washing facilities at the other end.

It could be used by those Ladies travelling in the Drawing-Room.

When she joined Trevor again, she said:

"I wish we were grand enough to have a coach of our own. I believe it is one like this that Queen Victoria uses when she travels in France."

"I can see you are getting ideas above your station," Trevor teased.

As he spoke, other guests began to arrive.

At first came two men whom Trevor knew and who, he told Angela, were experienced horsemen.

"I am hoping we can ride to-morrow on His Lordship's race-course," one of them said.

"Is there a private race-course at Vaux?" Angela could not help asking.

"There is, and it is an exact replica of the course at Newmarket," the Gentleman replied. "The Marquis tries out all his horses himself before he enters them for a race."

"That sounds very sensible," Angela said.

"It sounds as if you are keen on racing," the Gentleman replied, "and, by the way, it seems very rude, but I did not catch your name when we were introduced."

"I do not think Sir Trevor said it very clearly," Angela answered, "but it is actually Angela."

"Is that all?"

"I am going to Vaux to be an Angel in the Marquis's Play, so that is my name and it is easy to remember."

"It would be impossible for anyone to forget you!" the Gentleman said gallantly.

As Angela looked at Trevor, she saw he was frowning.

She, therefore, did not talk, but lapsed into silence.

The rest of the party began to arrive.

The five Girls from the Gaiety were exactly what Angela expected.

They seemed to her to be even more beautiful off-stage than they were on.

She recognised two of them, as she had seen

them coming down the staircase.

They were dressed even more elegantly than she was, in gowns of silk that rustled when they moved.

There were feathers in their hats and the diamonds in their ears and round their necks and wrists glistened.

Two of the Girls were wearing evening dress and explained that they had not had time to change.

They looked elegant in chiffon glittering with diamanté and wearing velvet wraps edged with sable.

Angela suspected, therefore, that they wished to look outstanding.

The five gentlemen who had arrived with them were extremely attractive and were obviously very close friends.

As soon as everybody was aboard, there was the sound of the Guard blowing his whistle and the train steamed out of the Station.

The Marquis's guests were then served with champagne and a delicious supper.

There were so many delightful things to eat that Angela was sorry she had already had dinner with Trevor.

She noticed that everybody not only ate, but drank a great deal.

The laughter grew louder and the voices seemed to get higher with every mile they travelled.

Trevor was quiet, as if he did not want to draw attention to himself and Angela.

But she heard one man say to him:

"Have you seen our host's new stallions?"

"No, not yet," Trevor answered.

"They're fantastic," his friend remarked. "With Arabian blood in them, I bet they will beat every horse he owns now."

Angela thought this sounded very exciting, as she meant to go to the Marquis's stables at the first opportunity.

The journey took only an hour by train from London.

When they stopped at the Halt nearest to the Marquis's seat, there were six carriages waiting to take them to Vaux, also two brakes for their luggage and the servants.

Trevor got Angela into the second carriage.

They were joined by two of the Gentlemen.

There were stars in the sky and a half moon rising up behind the trees.

Angela wanted to look out of the window to see the countryside.

The Gentlemen who sat opposite, however, persisted in talking to her.

They paid her extravagant compliments which she was sure annoyed Trevor.

Because she had no wish to upset him, she talked as little as possible.

At the same time, she was aware that in the light of the lantern inside the carriage the Gentlemen seldom took their eyes off her face.

They arrived at Vaux.

Angela first saw the long rows of steps surmounted on either side by heraldic crests in stone.

It was then she realised that Vaux was going to be even more impressive than she had imagined.

There was a red carpet up which they walked and what seemed to be an army of servants to meet them.

The footmen all wore white wigs.

Their claret-coloured coats were ornamented with gold-crested buttons.

Ahead of her were the occupants of the first carriage.

Angela walked into the house.

She saw Greek statues, magnificent pictures, and a finely painted ceiling before the Butler led them across the Hall.

There were double doors which were opened by two footmen.

The Butler walked in to announce in stentorian tones:

"Your guests, My Lord, have arrived from London."

Angela had a quick glimpse of the huge crystal chandeliers glittering in the light of the candles that burned in them.

The room was enormous.

There seemed to be a crowd at the far end of it.

One of them detached himself from the rest to walk towards them.

Angela knew it was the Marquis.

He was, in fact, just as she had expected him to be.

He was tall and broad-shouldered, and there was something athletic about the way he walked.

He was also, without exception, the most handsome man she had ever seen.

Yet, as he came nearer she saw that while he was

smiling, there was somehow a cynical expression in his eyes.

While he welcomed his guests he was, in some way she could not explain to herself, at the same time contemptuous of them.

He held out his hand to the men and the five Gaiety Girls who had entered the room first.

Then he said to Trevor:

"Good-evening, Brooke. It is nice to see you here again."

His eyes had swept over the Gaiety Girls until, as he spoke to Trevor, he saw who was standing beside him.

For a moment he just stared.

Quickly Trevor said:

"I have a message from George Edwardes."

"A message?" the Marquis questioned as if he were hardly listening.

"He was extremely perturbed to learn last night that Lucy is very ill."

Now there was no doubt that Trevor had the Marquis's attention.

"Lucy is ill?" he repeated slowly.

"She was worse this morning," Trevor went on, "and George Edwardes has therefore sent you a substitute in the shape of Angela, to whom, of course, we are very grateful for accepting the invitation at the last minute."

The Marquis was staring at Angela.

As if the rest of the party was aware that something dramatic was taking place, they were silent.

For the moment no-one who had just entered the room moved.

Angela looked up at the Marquis.

He could see her face very clearly in the light from the chandeliers.

There was silence.

It was only for a few seconds, and yet to Angela it seemed as if it lasted for a long time.

Then the Marquis held out his hand.

"Thank you," he said, "I am more grateful than I can possibly say that you should agree to come to save the Play which I have planned for everybody to see to-morrow night."

Angela put her hand into the Marquis's and curtsied.

She felt his fingers tighten on hers.

She knew that, as Trevor would have said, they had taken the second fence "in style."

chapter four

AS the party drank champagne, the laughter and noise increased.

The Marquis walked across to where Trevor was sitting beside Angela.

"I want, Brooke," he said, "for you to see my new stallions."

"I am looking forward to it," Trevor replied.

The Marquis was just about to say something else, when the door opened and the Butler announced:

"Miss Sadie Vandebilt, M'Lord!"

The Marquis looked up in astonishment.

Into the Drawing-Room came a beautiful young girl, exceedingly well-dressed, with a self-assurance which was very American.

Seeing the Marquis, she ran towards him.

"Here I am, Cousin Shaun. I gather you were not expecting me."

"Indeed I was not," the Marquis replied. "What has happened?"

"I wrote to you from America, saying I must come to England to buy some horses for Papa, and there was no time for you to reply, but I was sure you would get the letter."

"It never arrived," the Marquis answered.

"I learned that was so when I found there was no carriage waiting for me in London and I went to your house, hoping to find you there."

"Surely you have not come alone?" the Marquis exclaimed.

Sadie Vandebilt laughed.

"Alone, except for Aunt Chrissie who, as you know, is Papa's sister; and a Courier, a Detective, and two lady's-maids."

The Marquis laughed.

"You were certainly well protected!"

Sadie Vandebilt looked at him mischievously.

"Aunt Chrissie went to bed feeling sea-sick while we were still in New York Harbour, and she would speak to nobody all the way over. She is now in bed at your house."

The Marquis laughed again before he said:

"Anyway, you are here."

"I came with your coachman and a most marvellous team of chestnuts. It took two hours and twenty minutes. I do hope that is a record!"

"Very nearly," the Marquis said. "And at least you have arrived safely."

As he spoke, there came a burst of laughter from the Gaiety Girls and their admirers, who were standing in front of the fireplace.

Angela saw the expression in his eyes.

She knew that he was, in fact, perturbed at

his cousin's unexpected arrival at this particular moment.

Quickly, as if to divert her attention from what was happening, the Marquis said:

"If you have come to buy horses, let me introduce you to Sir Trevor Brooke. He is an expert on horse-flesh and I promise you can trust his judgement on whatever you buy."

"I will certainly do my best," Trevor said.

He held out his hand, and Sadie Vandebilt shook it.

"I want at least ten fine race-horses," she said, "several stallions, and a large number of brood mares."

Watching them, Angela saw the excitement in Trevor's eyes and knew what this would mean to him.

"What I suggest, Brooke," the Marquis interrupted, "is that you give my cousin some champagne and, of course, talk about horses while I look after Angela."

Angela thought he was about to introduce her to Sadie Vandebilt.

Instead, he drew her to one side, saying:

"What would you like to do?"

"If it is not rude," Angela replied, "I am very tired and I would like to go to bed."

"Then of course that is what you must do," the Marquis agreed.

He walked towards the door, and Angela took a quick glance at her brother.

He was, however, absorbed in conversation with the American girl.

Without speaking to him, she therefore hurried after the Marquis.

They walked across the Hall and she thought he would leave her at the bottom of the stairs.

Instead, he said:

"I will show you to your room and, of course, when I have an opportunity, show you how grateful I am that you have come to take Lucy's place in my Play."

He smiled, and then continued:

"We will have our first rehearsal to-morrow morning. You must let me give you something you really want so that I can show my gratitude."

"There is no need for that," Angela replied.

"There is every need for it," the Marquis contradicted, "and I shall not allow you to refuse."

Angela drew in her breath.

They were half-way up the stairs when she stopped.

"If you really mean what you say," she said, "I can tell you now exactly what I want."

"Then, of course, I must give it to you," the Marquis replied, "together with my most heartfelt thanks."

His words were light, but there was a somewhat hard expression in his eyes.

He thought the newcomer might look like an Angel, but she was certainly very down-to-earth when it came to material things.

He wondered cynically if she would ask for diamonds, or if she would leave the choice of stones to him.

"What I would like, if you will give it to me,"

Angela said, "is your permission to . . . ride one of your . . . new stallions."

The Marquis stared at her.

"Ride one of my new stallions?" he repeated. "Are you a good rider?"

"Without boasting," Angela replied, "I have ridden ever since I could walk, and my father, when he was alive, was very proud of me."

The Marquis looked at her searchingly as if he found it hard to believe what she was saying.

Then he answered:

"Very well, but I must warn you, Angela, they are very spirited and hard to hold."

"That is exactly what I hoped they would be," Angela replied.

They walked to the top of the stairs, along the corridor that contained fine pieces of furniture.

Angela was aware there were also some exquisite pictures on the walls.

They were nearly at the end of it when the Marquis stopped outside a door that was half-open.

"This is the room in which you are sleeping," he said.

Angela did not know that it was the room he had chosen for Lucy.

As she had not arrived, the Housekeeper had naturally prepared it for the girl who was taking her place.

There was a housemaid unpacking the few things that remained in one of Angela's trunks.

She rose when the Marquis appeared, dropped him a curtsy, and tactfully left the room.

It was a very impressive bedroom.

The huge four-poster had a gilded canopy of Cupids holding garlands.

The thick posts had carved on them small birds fluttering amongst the foliage of a tree.

"I think you will be comfortable here," the Marquis said, "and there is a Boudoir next door."

He walked across to a door near the window and opened it.

Because he seemed to expect it, Angela followed him.

She saw there was a beautifully furnished Sitting-Room filled with flowers whose fragrance scented the air.

It was lit by several small candelabra that stood on the mantelpiece and on side tables.

"What a beautiful room!" she exclaimed.

"That is what I have always thought," the Marquis replied, "and my room is beyond it."

He walked back into the bedroom as he spoke, and said:

"Now I will leave you to get some sleep, and if you are awake to-morrow morning, I will let you ride one of my stallions at seven-thirty. Then immediately after breakfast we must rehearse the part you are to take in my Play before we start the races which I have planned to take place after an early Luncheon."

"It sounds very exciting," Angela exclaimed. "I am afraid it will be impossible for me to sleep in case I miss any of it."

The Marquis laughed.

Then, to her surprise, he took her hand and raised it to his lips.

"Thank you once again for coming," he said.

Before Angela could answer, he had left the room and the housemaid came back to finish the unpacking.

Although she thought she would not sleep, Angela was very tired after all that had happened during the day.

She fell asleep as soon as her head touched the pillow.

Angela had instructed the housemaid to call her at six forty-five A.M.

When the maid did so, she jumped out of bed and put on one of the riding-habits which Nelly had lent her.

She went downstairs just before the hand of the Grandfather clock in the Hall touched seven-thirty.

She was not surprised to find that the Marquis was already there.

He looked up as she approached and said:

"You are punctual, which is unusual in a woman, and, of course, very smart!"

Angela thought he was being sarcastic.

She was well aware that her riding-habit would have been considered outrageous on any hunting-field.

"I thought, as we were riding so early," she said in a low voice, "there was no need to put on the hat that matches this habit, which makes me feel very over-dressed."

"I doubt if there will be anyone to admire you at this time of the morning, except myself," the Marquis answered.

She thought there was a mocking note in his voice.

She wished she were not wearing the pale green habit which Nelly had chosen for her.

Then she told herself she would certainly be a laughing-stock in the only habit she possessed, as it was threadbare.

Also having been bought when she was younger, it was really too tight for her.

As they reached the top of the steps outside the front-door, the horses were being brought round.

Once Angela saw the two stallions, she forgot everything in her excitement at being able to ride one of the finest horses she had ever seen.

They were both being rather frisky.

She knew, as the Marquis helped her into the saddle, that he was worried in case she had been over-confident.

Then she told herself he was not worried about her but whether she would be thrown.

In consequence, she might be unable to take the part of the Angel in his Play.

As she took up the reins, she began to talk to the horse in a soft voice.

Leaning forward to pat his neck, she told him how fine he was and how much she enjoyed riding him.

It was her father who had taught her to talk to a horse she was riding for the first time.

As she did so, she moved away from the front of the house.

By the time the Marquis had mounted his own horse and followed her, Angela was some way down the drive.

As he came alongside her, he heard her saying:

"You are very beautiful, so beautiful that I want you to show me exactly what you can do and if you can jump higher than any other horse I have ever ridden."

"You are being over-optimistic," the Marquis said as he came closer, "if you think I will allow you to jump."

Angela did not answer.

At the same time, her eyes were twinkling.

She told herself that if she had the chance, it would be difficult for him to stop her.

They had gone a little way down the drive, when the Marquis turned.

Passing through some trees, Angela found herself on flat land where the stallion could gallop.

She did not wait for the Marquis to suggest it.

She set off so quickly that it surprised him.

He had to push his own horse forward to catch up with her.

The two stallions were delighted to race each other.

They went at such a speed that Angela was glad she was not wearing a hat.

She was certain it would have been blown away.

As it was, although she had pinned her hair tightly to her head, there were little tendrils curling round her forehead.

After galloping for nearly a mile, they pulled in their horses.

As they did so, she said breathlessly:

"Thank you, thank you! That was the most marvellous ride I have had for a long time!"

"I need not tell you that you sit a horse magnificently," the Marquis said. "I cannot understand why, looking as you do, you do not have a hundred horses at your disposal."

For a moment Angela did not understand what he meant.

Then she realised that what he was implying was that if she was a Gaiety Girl, there would be plenty of men like himself who would allow her to ride their horses.

She thought it was a difficult question to answer.

She therefore said:

"May I look at your race-course? I hear it is an exact replica of the course at Newmarket."

"I suppose Brooke told you that," the Marquis said, "and I am very proud of it. I would like you to see it, although you will do so after Luncheon."

"What exactly is happening this afternoon?" Angela enquired.

"I thought it would amuse your friend Brooke and the other men staying in the house to race some of my horses," the Marquis replied. "I have also invited a number of neighbours who are as keen as I am in building up their stables."

"It sounds thrilling!" Angela said.

"I do not think you will find the Ladies eager to take part, but, of course, you may ride in the flat race if you want to."

"That would be marvellous, if I can ride your horses," Angela replied.

"They are at your disposal," the Marquis said, "with the exception of *Saracen*, whom you are riding now, for the simple reason that I am keeping him for the Steeple-Chase we will have at the end."

They reached the race-course.

Angela stared at it, thinking it was very cleverly built on a flat piece of land.

It was protected on two sides by woods, which made it very sheltered.

The race-course, being on the same lines as the Newmarket course, meant quite a strenuous ride if one was to go round it three times.

She could see that in the centre of it there were movable fences which could be put into place for the Steeple-Chase.

"It is very clever of you," Angela said, "to have thought of such a convenient way of exercising and training your horses."

"That is what I thought myself," the Marquis said, "and you can see that I have had the fences specially constructed so that they move with ease over the course without damaging the ground."

"Do show me how it is done," Angela begged.

There were men already working on the course.

The Marquis rode up and ordered them to pull out one of the fences.

A man obeyed him, and Angela could see how skilfully the fence had been made and that it was very high.

In fact, she guessed it was as high as some of those that were on the Grand National Course at Aintree.

The man set the fence in place and stood back so that she and the Marquis could see it.

"You need to be very experienced to take this sort of fence," the Marquis was saying in an authoritative tone. "In fact, I am sure you realise, Angela, that you need to start preparing for the jump some distance before your horse reaches it."

"I think I understand what you mean," Angela replied.

As she spoke, she moved *Saracen* into the centre of the race-course.

She looked ahead, following exactly what the Marquis was saying.

"I think most of the men who are here this afternoon will be able to manage these jumps," he went on, "and certainly they will not prove too difficult for your friend, Trevor, who is an outstanding equestrian."

"That is what I have always thought," Angela agreed.

Then, as she saw the Marquis was about to order the men to remove the fences, she urged *Saracen* forward.

It was some seconds before the Marquis realised what she was doing.

Then, as he shouted: "No, Angela, stop!" it was too late.

She touched *Saracen* with her heels and he knew exactly what was required of him.

He sailed over the fence with at least six inches to spare.

She landed on the other side and rode some distance down the course before she turned *Saracen* round.

The Marquis was now a long way from her, and she felt sure as she rode *Saracen* once again at the fence that he was shouting for her not to do so.

Saracen jumped as he had before, and they landed without any difficulty.

Angela rode up to the Marquis.

As she reached him, she realised he was not looking at her admiringly as she had hoped, but angrily.

"How dare you do that," he said, "when I had told you not to!"

"I am sorry," Angela said, "but it was a challenge I could not resist. Please, do not be cross with me."

She looked so lovely and in a way so childlike as she spoke that unexpectedly the Marquis laughed.

"I do not believe you are an Angel," he said, "but a small devil from Hell who has no right to be here, giving me a heart-attack!"

"I am quite unharmed," Angela replied, "and so is *Saracen*. He would like to tell you that he enjoyed every minute of it!"

"I am sure he did," the Marquis said grimly, "but you are not, and on this I will be obeyed, to enter for the Steeple-Chase this afternoon."

There was silence.

Then Angela said:

"I would like to say that I think you are very unsporting, but I suppose I should be grateful for small mercies, and thank you for letting me ride *Saracen* in the first place."

The Marquis laughed again.

"You are definitely determined to try the patience of a Saint!" he said. "And while I can see, Angela, that you ride better than any woman I have ever met, I am not going to risk being beaten on my own race-course by a woman!"

This time it was Angela who laughed.

"I understand," she said, "and of course I would hate to do anything that might topple you from your perch!"

The Marquis turned his horse towards the house.

"You have given me enough heart-attacks for one morning," he said. "Now we will go and have some breakfast and after that we will see if you have as much flair for acting as you do for horse-riding."

Angela did not reply, and after a moment he said:

"I have not yet been told where you have come from. I know it is not from George Edwardes, or I would have seen you at the Gaiety."

"As I do not wish to worry you unnecessarily," Angela replied, "I think I will answer that question after we have had our rehearsal, and not before."

She thought the Marquis might argue with her, so she put *Saracen* into a trot and going ahead the way they had come, rode towards the drive.

The grooms were waiting at the door to take away the horses.

Angela patted *Saracen* and thanked him for being so good.

As they walked up the steps and through the front-door, she said to the Marquis:

"Is it all right for me to come into the Dining-Room dressed as I am?"

"I am sure, as it is so early, there will be no-one there to pay you compliments," the Marquis answered somewhat sarcastically.

He thought as he spoke that it was unusual for a

woman to be so unselfconscious about her looks.

He had noticed the way that Angela had pushed back her wind-swept hair with her hand.

The other Gaiety Girls would also have powdered their noses and reddened their lips.

It suddenly struck him that in fact Angela had not used any cosmetics before she came riding.

Apparently the fact had never occurred to her.

Only the Marquis knew that it was very unusual for any young woman who was constantly in front of the public to appear without her make-up.

As he had predicted, although breakfast was ready, there was no-one in the Dining-Room

There was a long array of silver entree dishes on the sideboard with candle flames beneath them.

It made Angela think of the days when she had been little and her Father and Mother had entertained for the Hunt Ball or the parties they gave in the Summer.

Then there had been a Butler and three footmen to wait on the guests.

Breakfast had been arranged in exactly the same way as it was here, and the guests had helped themselves.

"Would you like fish or eggs?" the Marquis asked, raising the lids of the entree dishes one by one.

"As I am hungry, I think I will have both!" Angela replied.

He helped her to fish and eggs and she sat down at the table, pouring herself out a cup of coffee from the coffee-pot.

The Marquis had just joined her, when the door opened and Trevor came in.

"Good-morning, My Lord!" he said to the Marquis, then to Angela:

"I guessed when I went to your room and found it empty that you had gone riding."

"It has been the most exciting thing I have ever done," Angela said, "and having seen the Marquis's stallions before you have done so, I can tell you they are magnificent!"

"I hope you rode well," Trevor remarked.

"I did not disgrace you, if that is what you are implying," Angela replied.

They were talking to each other as they always did.

Then, as if Trevor suddenly remembered they were supposed to be something other than brother and sister, he put a hand on her shoulder and said:

"I should have been very worried if the horses had been too much for you, or you had had a fall."

For a moment Angela stared at him.

Then, when she understood, she answered:

"It is sweet of you to worry, but there is no need. I have come back to you intact."

"Of course that is all I want," Trevor said.

Angela wanted to giggle at the way they were behaving.

She only hoped the Marquis was impressed.

Then, as Trevor helped himself from the dishes on the sideboard, two other men appeared and there was no need for Angela to go on talking.

She had a second helping of breakfast as well as enjoying several pieces of toast spread with Jersey butter and comb honey.

It was very different from the meagre meals she had been having recently, when she was lucky if they could afford one small egg.

'If I were a camel,' she thought, 'I would be able to stuff myself with this delicious food and go without any more for at least a week!'

It was an amusing thought.

Her eyes must have been twinkling, for the man next to her said:

"You are looking very happy! Has anyone particularly pleased you in this party, or have I got a chance of looking in?"

It took Angela a second or two to understand what he was implying.

Then she replied:

"I am afraid the answer to that is 'No.' I have fallen madly in love, and his name is *Saracen!*"

For a moment the man who had spoken looked perplexed.

But the Marquis understood and, as she rose to leave the room, he rose, too, to open the door.

As he did so, he said:

"The Gentleman you love will be waiting for you this afternoon."

"Then I will be pleased to see him," Angela said. "I am going to change now. Where shall I meet you?"

"Ask one of the footmen to take you to my Theatre," the Marquis replied.

Angela smiled at him, then hurried away to take off her riding-habit.

She put on one of the pretty gowns which Nelly had given her.

Her maid tidied her hair, and for the first time she remembered that she should use the cosmetics that had been unpacked and put into a drawer of the dressing-table.

Somewhat tentatively she put a little powder on her nose and chin.

Then she reddened her lips.

It made her look, she thought, somehow unlike herself.

At the same time, she look theatrical and she hoped that was what the Marquis would think.

Because she was still flushed from riding, it seemed unnecessary to put any colour on her cheeks.

She ran down to the Hall to find three footmen on duty.

She asked one of them to take her to His Lordship's Theatre.

"You'll admire it, Miss, when you sees it," he said as he walked along the corridor. "Everyone says it be the finest private Theatre in t'whole country!"

The way he spoke told Angela he was very proud of serving anyone who had anything so exceptional.

He opened the door with a flourish, and when she looked inside she could understand why he was impressed.

Compared to an ordinary Theatre, it was small.

Yet Angela could understand that it was large compared to some of the private Theatres she had read about.

It was built to hold fifty people sitting in the comfortable armchairs in the Stalls.

There were several boxes draped with velvet curtains.

So palatial was it that it seemed almost a shame that so few people could see anything as spectacular

There was a small Orchestra Pit, and the stage was fashioned exactly in the traditional style with footlights.

The crimson velvet curtains were sumptuous and embellished with tassels.

As Angela stood and stared, the curtains were drawn back.

It was then she saw that the stage was arranged for what she thought must be the first scene in "The Rake's Progress."

She was looking at it admiringly, when the Marquis came up behind her and asked:

"Well? What do you think of my Theatre?"

"You know without my saying so that it is magnificent!" Angela answered. "I was told you had copied it from the Theatre in the Winter Palace in St. Petersburg."

"I copied the structure," the Marquis replied, "but the decoration is entirely my own."

"It is beautiful, like everything else in your house," Angela said.

She looked towards the stage.

"Is that a scene from 'The Rake's Progress'?"

"I suppose Brooke told you what I was doing," the Marquis replied, "but I am having a different ending, which is where you come in."

"You mean the Angel is going to save him from Bedlam," Angela answered. "Oh, I am so glad! It has always made me sad to think of him there, regretting everything he has lost."

The Marquis looked at her in astonishment.

"You seem to know a great deal about 'The Rake's Progress,' or was it Brooke who told you?"

"My father had eight prints of 'The Rake's Progress,'" Angela explained, "and therefore I have always been interested in Hogarth."

"So you know why he became famous?" the Marquis asked.

"Of course I do," Angela replied. "It was because he decided to paint pictures with a moral to them. In that way he became one of the most notable men of his day."

"You surprise me," the Marquis remarked.

"Why?" Angela asked.

Without him replying, she knew it was because he was thinking of her as if she were one of the Gaiety Girls.

She had already realised that they were very beautiful, very attractive, and could flirt in a manner which would have shocked her mother.

But they were none of them well-educated.

She had heard them talking on the train and in the Drawing-Room last night.

She knew then that her Mother and Father would not approve of her pretending to be one of them.

Because it was something she did not wish to discuss, she said quickly:

"Now, please tell me exactly what I am to do."

The Marquis took her up onto the stage.

"This is the first scene," he said, "in which obviously you do not appear. I have cut the story down to three scenes. I decided the most effective would be 'The Rake's Levee,' and of course the glamorous women will be played by the Gaiety Girls. Then the Gambling House where he loses all his money. After that you rescue him from the Debtor's Prison."

"How do I do that?" Angela asked.

The Marquis explained how the Rake would first be jeered at by the other inmates, who would all be uncouth men and not Gentlemen, as the Rake was supposed to be.

"He will then die," the Marquis said finally, "but you will come down from Heaven to tell him that if he is sorry for his sins, you will take him to Paradise from where he can come back and be given a second chance to be a successful man instead of a complete and utter failure."

The Marquis spoke slowly, as if he were speaking to a child.

Angela clasped her hands together.

"I like that!" she approved. "Now I can feel happy about the poor Rake. He has always worried me because his life was so futile, and he threw away his money in a foolish and reckless manner."

"As a great many men do!" the Marquis said cynically. "Are you sorry for all of them too?"

"I am sorry for anybody who misses the chance of living life to the fullest," Angela answered. "Life is difficult, and we all go through unhappy experiences, not always of our own making. But if we have courage, we can survive."

She was thinking of Trevor and herself as she spoke, and her voice was very moving.

"Is that what you have done?" the Marquis asked.

She had forgotten to whom she was speaking, and for a moment she could not think of an answer.

Then she said:

"Yes, it is true. But I do not want to talk about that."

"Very well," the Marquis agreed. "Let us start rehearsing."

He lay down on the stage as he would have if he were in Prison.

He handed Angela the script with her lines on it.

There were not many, and as she had a good memory, she was word-perfect after the first time she had repeated them.

They went over it several times before the Marquis said:

"I can see what you are doing moves you and, as you feel for the unhappy Rake, I do not want to rehearse you anymore."

"Why not?" Angela asked.

"Because I am afraid it will spoil the spontaneity of it," he replied. "In fact, Angela, you are so good that I am suspicious you are not only an outstanding rider, but also, unknown to me, a distinguished actress!"

Angela laughed.

"That is what I would like to be at this moment, but thank you for the compliment."

"You should be used to them by now," the Marquis remarked.

"I doubt if you will believe me," Angela replied, "but I had received very few before last night."

"If that is really true, what did you think of them?" the Marquis enquired.

"To be honest, I thought they were too slick and had been repeated so often that they no longer sounded sincere."

The Marquis laughed.

"You cannot be a cynic at your age!" he said. "I am sure the Gentlemen who paid you compliments would be horrified at what you have just said."

"Then, please, do not tell them," Angela answered, "but when you ask me questions I find myself automatically telling you the truth."

"Are you telling me you never lie?" the Marquis asked.

It flashed through Angela's mind that she was, in fact, acting a lie at this moment, and a very big one.

"I did not say that," she said after a moment's pause, "but I know it is a great mistake to lie unless one absolutely has to. It is wrong and sometimes even wicked to do so."

The Marquis glanced at her before he said:

"When we have time, which is not at this moment, as we must get back to the others, I want to talk to you, Angela, about what you think is good and what you think is wicked. Let me tell you, and this is not a compliment, that you look good."

"That is what I have tried to be all my life," Angela answered. "I have always felt it was a responsibility to look like an Angel."

She did not see the expression in the Marquis's eyes as they walked from the Theatre back towards the centre of the house.

He did not speak until they heard the noise of

voices in the Drawing-Room.

The rest of the house-party had come downstairs and were doubtless drinking champagne before their early Luncheon.

Angela, however, because she was going to be allowed to ride, went upstairs to change.

She was glad that Nelly had been so particular as to provide her with two riding-habits.

Now she could wear the blue one which she thought was the prettiest and which the Marquis had not seen before.

She asked if the other Ladies were wearing hats at Luncheon.

"Yes, Miss," the maid replied. "They're all ready to get into brakes, which'll take them to the race-course. 'Is Lordship gets cross if 'e's kep' waitin'."

Angela, therefore, put on the blue riding-hat with its gauze veil.

When she looked at herself in the mirror, she thought she looked very unlike the Angel and exactly like a Gaiety Girl.

"Papa would be horrified at my appearance," she told her reflection, and for one moment felt afraid.

Then she remembered the thousand pounds that was going to repair the roof of the Priory.

As if to force herself to play the part for which she was being paid, she powdered her face again and put on more lipstick.

Then with her head held high, she walked down the stairs.

She was telling herself that nothing mattered except that she and Trevor should get away without anyone guessing their secret!

chapter five

THE Marquis's plans went, as might have been expected, exactly as he wanted.

The races which Angela found thrilling were faster and more proficient than anything she had ever seen.

She took part in one race in which, to her delight, she came in third.

The Marquis was first and Trevor, riding a magnificent horse belonging to him, was second.

Angela was only half a length behind.

She received many congratulations from the men.

She thought, however, the women who were not taking part looked rather sour.

Three of the Gaiety Girls rode, but not very well.

The others said they would be spectators.

A number of men, who Angela learned were the Marquis's neighbours, arrived to take part in the races.

They had fine horses, but nothing to equal his.

Half-way through the afternoon, when Angela was resting after her race, a voice beside her said:

"I have found you again, pretty lady!"

She looked up and saw it was Lord Grentham.

She looked at him in surprise.

"Why are you here?" she enquired.

"Because," he replied, "I am riding one of my horses which I intend to race against the Marquis's and I am coming to see your performance to-night."

He paused, smiled at her, and continued:

"I know you will look even more beautiful than you do now."

It was not what he said but the way that he said it which made Angela feel uncomfortable.

There was something too familiar in his voice and the way he looked at her.

She felt as if she were being insulted.

Then she remembered that she was not Angela Brooke, but an unknown young woman who associated with Gaiety Girls.

She thought, too, that the compliments she had been paid since she had arrived at Vaux were given in very much the same way.

She told herself that for the first time in her life she was being treated as if she were not a Lady.

To her consternation, Lord Grentham sat down beside her on the brake and said:

"I want you to tell me all about yourself. The moment I saw you I realised you were what I have been looking for all my life."

"I really have nothing to tell," Angela said.

"Nonsense!" he replied. "You have lived for nineteen—or is it twenty—years, and I want you to tell me who are your parents, where you live, and who brought you to London."

Angela did not answer, and he went on:

"I cannot believe it was Brooke, as I hear he has very little money and could not afford anything so ravishing and so exquisite as you!"

Angela looked around her.

She could see Trevor talking, as she might have expected, to Sadie Vandebilt.

He was being very attentive.

Angela was intelligent enough to know that he was deliberately preventing her from associating with the Gaiety Girls.

At this moment, however, she wanted to run to her brother to beg him to look after her.

She did not know why, but she thought Lord Grentham was menacing her.

She thought, too, that he might be a danger if he exposed her as being a fraud.

It would certainly hurt Trevor.

She rose from her seat, and Lord Grentham asked:

"Where are you going?"

"I want to speak to our host about the horses," Angela said.

Climbing down from the brake, she walked quickly away.

She thought if she was going to the Marquis, it was unlikely that Lord Grentham would follow her.

Although she did not look back, she was sure he had not done so.

She found the Marquis instructing the men, as he had done before, how to erect the jumps for the Steeple-Chase.

Because she felt Lord Grentham was watching her, she went up and stood beside him.

After a moment the Marquis asked:

"What is it, Angela? If you have come to ask me if you may ride *Saracen*, the answer is 'No.' I intend to ride him myself."

"Then you will undoubtedly win," Angela said, "but I came to ask you for something else."

"What is it?" he enquired.

She thought he was finding her a nuisance, and she said quickly:

"It does not matter. I will tell you later."

She walked away before he could stop her.

She thought the mere fact that she had been speaking to him might prevent Lord Grentham approaching her immediately.

But she was over-optimistic.

The minute he saw her leave the Marquis, he jumped down from the brake and came to her side.

"Now that your business with our host is over," he said, "I would like you to come and look at my horse and tell me if you think he is better than any of the Marquis's."

Because it was difficult to think of an excuse, Angela allowed him to lead her to where his horse was standing.

He was being held by a groom and was a very fine stallion.

Although she wanted to find fault, it was difficult to do so.

She patted the horse, and Lord Grentham said:

"If you ask me nicely, I will let you ride any of my horses that you wish. I am sure you would cause a sensation in Hyde Park!"

"That will be difficult, as I am not going to London," Angela replied.

Lord Grentham looked at her.

"What do you mean—you are not going to London?"

"Exactly what I say. When I leave here, I am going back to the country."

"And where is that?"

"Nowhere that you would know and, quite frankly, I do not encourage visitors."

"You are very elusive," Lord Grentham said. "What is your game? Are you setting your cap at Vauxhall? Because if you are, you are wasting your time."

Angela thought this was definitely insulting.

She therefore put her head in the air and walked away.

She had gone only a few steps before Lord Grentham caught hold of her arm.

"Now, do not dare to leave me," he said. "I have gone to a great deal of trouble to get myself invited here to-day, just to see you again. I have a suggestion to put to you as to your future, which I think will interest you."

"You are wrong," Angela said coldly. "My future is already planned, and therefore there is no point in discussing it."

"There is every point!" Lord Grentham said angrily. "To put it bluntly, Angela, I want you and I intend to have you! And in case no-one has told you so, I will inform you that am a very rich man."

Angela drew in her breath.

She had no idea that men like Lord Grentham talked so bluntly to the sort of young woman she was pretending to be.

She was wondering where she could run to.

Then she saw the Marquis walking away from a hedge he had been inspecting.

Quickly she shook herself free of Lord Grentham's grasp and ran towards him.

He noticed as she reached him that she was looking upset.

Before she could speak, he asked:

"What is the matter? Are you having trouble with Grentham?"

"He will not . . . leave me alone," Angela stammered. "And . . . he frightens me!"

The Marquis looked at Lord Grentham, who had stopped walking after Angela.

Instead, he was staring at the race-course.

"I will deal with him," the Marquis said. "He has always been a nuisance, and I have no liking for him. I will tell him to leave you alone."

"Thank you . . . thank you!" Angela said. "I am . . . sorry . . . to be a . . . bother."

The Marquis smiled.

"It is no bother, and I will not have you upset when you have to look like an Angel and behave like one."

"That is what I am trying to do," Angela answered.

"This is the last race," the Marquis said, "and as soon as it is over, we will all go back to the house. If you take my advice, you will go and lie down and rest before the performance."

"I will do that," Angela answered, "and . . . thank you."

"You can thank me later," he replied.

He walked on towards the horses.

Angela was praying that Lord Grentham would not approach her again now that she was alone.

Hurriedly she talked to two men to whom she had been introduced at Luncheon.

They were not taking part in the Steeple-Chase, and were quite happy to discuss with her the finer points of the horses that were.

She managed to stay with them until the race had started.

It was very exciting, and the horses jumped superbly.

She was thrilled when *Saracen* won.

Then, as soon as the race was over, she got into the brake with the other girls.

They drove back to the house.

As the Marquis had suggested, she went up to her room and the maid brought her a cup of tea.

"I've got your gown ready for to-night, Miss," the maid said, "and ever so pretty it is!"

Angela had forgotten until then that the Marquis had told her she was having a special gown to wear and would not require one of her own.

When she saw it, she realised how clever he had been in choosing something that was exactly right for the part.

It was simple, made of chiffon, and attached to it cleverly so that the bands did not show were the two wings.

They were made of swans' feathers.

Angela thought they were exactly what an Angel would wear.

There was also a small halo of iridescent stones to wear at the back of her head.

She had been told to be backstage by six-thirty, as the performance was to start a quarter of an hour later.

Angela started dressing early, just in case at the last minute there was anything wrong with her gown.

When the halo had been fixed securely, the maid said:

"Excuse me, Miss, for suggestin' it, but Lady Mary's bin beggin' to see you ever since she heard there's an Angel in th' Play."

"Lady Mary?" Angela questioned.

She wondered if Lady Mary was an elderly relative of the Marquis's whom she had not met.

"It's 'is Lordship's daughter," the maid said.

"His daughter?" Angela exclaimed. "I had no idea the Marquis was married."

" 'E was, Miss, but 'is wife died havin' a baby. Ever so sad it was. I always thinks as 'ow Lady Mary misses the mother she never knew."

"How old is Lady Mary?" Angela enquired.

"She's six, Miss, ever so pretty, an' she does want to see you!"

"Then of course I will see her," Angela agreed.

She glanced in the mirror.

"I am ready now, so perhaps you can take me to her."

"You're not goin' to wear any make-up, Miss?" the maid suggested.

Angela shook her head.

"No. I think it is wrong for an Angel."

She thought, as she spoke, of what her Mother had told her about Angels when she was a child.

They had certainly not painted their lips red, or powdered their noses for that matter.

She glanced at the clock and saw there was plenty of time.

The maid took her up to the next floor.

As they went up the stairs, Angela asked:

"Does Lady Mary have a Governess?"

"No, Miss," the maid replied. "She takes her lessons with the Vicar's little daughter, but she's still got Nanny. As it 'appens, Nanny's away to-night on account of 'er mother being ill. One of the 'ousemaids is lookin' after Lady Mary."

By this time they had reached the next floor.

The maid opened a door into what was a very large and attractive Nursery.

It contained the same things Angela had known as a child.

There was a rocking-horse and a screen covered with amusing stickers and Christmas cards.

In a corner of the room stood a large dolls'-house.

The room, however, was empty, and the maid went to another door and said:

"Are you there, Your Ladyship? I've brought th' Angel to see you!"

There was a cry of delight, and a moment later

a little girl wearing her nightgown came running into the Nursery.

She was a very pretty child with brown curly hair and large blue eyes in a little pointed face.

Angela was standing in front of the fireplace, and she stopped in front of her to ask:

"You really are an Angel and you have wings?"

"Yes, I have wings," Angela answered.

She turned round so that the child could see them.

She touched them very gently with her fingers and said:

"They are made of feathers!"

"Of course they are," Angela said, "and I expect real Angels have feathers just like them, taken from the swans which fly through the clouds to reach Heaven."

"I have seen swans flying," Lady Mary said. "Is that where they go?"

"I think all birds when they fly up into the sky are looking for Heaven," Angela said. "I used to watch the swans when I was a little girl and when they disappeared into the clouds, I was sure they were with the Angels."

"That is what I think too," Lady Mary said. "Please may I touch your halo?"

Angela knelt down so that the child could touch it with gentle fingers.

"It is very pretty," she said, "and it means that you are very, very good."

"Of course it does," Angela agreed, "and that is what I try to be."

She thought this was a strange conversation to

be having with a child after what she had said to her Father.

"I must go now," she said, "because if I am late, your Daddy will be angry."

"You will come back again?" Lady Mary begged.

"Of course I will," Angela said. "I did not know you were here until Emily told me."

She looked at the maid as she spoke.

"I am not allowed downstairs when Daddy has his noisy parties," Lady Mary said. "When I asked him if I could come down and see his Play, he said 'No.' "

It was obvious that this had hurt the little girl's feelings, and Angela said quickly:

"I am sure he will put on another Play, perhaps at Christmas, which you will enjoy more than this one."

"I would like to see you because you are an Angel," Lady Mary said positively.

"When I come and see you to-morrow I will tell you about the Play," Angela answered.

"Come and see me to-night," Lady Mary begged. "Daddy will not come because he is busy and I shall be all alone."

Because she sounded so pathetic, Angela said:

"I think you will be asleep, but I promise you I will come up and say good-night after the Play when I, too, will be going to bed."

"You promise? You promise?" Lady Mary asked.

"I promise!" Angela said solemnly. "But try to go to sleep and to-morrow we will talk about everything."

"I would like that," Lady Mary said, "but I am not allowed downstairs."

"That does not matter," Angela said, "because I will come up to you."

Lady Mary put her arms round Angela's neck and kissed her.

"Thank you," she said. "Now that I have kissed an Angel, perhaps I will become one too."

"Of course you will, someday," Angela replied, "but not until you are very old and have had lots of things happen to you in your life."

"What sort of things?" Lady Mary asked curiously.

"I will tell you about them to-morrow," Angela promised.

She rose from her knees as she spoke, and Lady Mary said again:

"Promise you will come and say good-night to me."

"I promise," Angela said. "Now I must hurry because your Daddy will be waiting for me."

She walked towards the door, turned back to wave, and Lady Mary waved to her.

As she went down the stairs, she thought it was strange that the Marquis had a daughter whom he had never mentioned.

She wondered if Trevor knew he had been married.

There was, however, no time for speculation.

Emily the maid hurried her down the passages, where she would not be seen until they reached the back door of the Theatre.

As soon as she entered, Angela could hear the

chatter and laughter of the audience.

She was aware that they were mostly the men who had been taking part in the races.

There were, however, some women amongst them, and she was able to peep at them through the side of the curtain.

She knew at a glance they were not the sort of women her Mother would have welcomed.

She suspected the men with them treated them in the same way that they treated the Gaiety Girls.

She was aware that the small Theatre was almost full.

It was then she heard the Marquis say:

"Come away from there, Angela. We are going to start, and we must all be ready to take our cue."

As he spoke, there was music from the Orchestra.

Angela moved back, as she could see the curtain rising to reveal the set on which they had rehearsed in the morning.

The first scene was, she realised, the second of Hogarth's pictures, which he had entitled "The Rake's Levee."

The Marquis, as the Rake, looking incredibly smart, was entertaining his friends.

They were, Angela realised, the five Gaiety Girls and the five men who had come down from London with them.

There was music during the "Levee" and a lot of champagne to drink.

The conversation, which had been written by the Marquis, was witty and amusing.

It kept the audience laughing until, when the

Rake had obviously had too much to drink, the curtain fell.

There was enthusiastic applause.

The five Gaiety Girls walked onto the stage to sing a song that was a hit in "Cinder-Ellen Up-to-Date."

Their voices were not particularly outstanding, but they looked extremely pretty.

When the song ended, they danced round, showing their legs as they swirled and kicked.

Their efforts evoked rapturous applause from the audience.

As the song finished and they moved away, the lights went down.

The curtain rose on what Angela realised was a Gaming House.

For a moment Hogarth's picture was depicted very clearly.

The Rake was handing over his winnings to attractive women who kept asking for more.

Finally he had nothing left.

He then went down on his knees and raised his hands in despair just as Hogarth had painted the Rake.

The curtain fell while the scene was changed.

One of the Marquis's friends walked on stage to sing a song which was very popular in the Music Halls.

It was called "Champagne Charlie."

Wearing a top-hat and carrying a cane, the man performed very well and had a good baritone voice.

Because it was such a popular song, everybody knew it.

He persuaded the audience to sing with him until the small Theatre rang with the sound.

There was a tremendous applause at the end and then, for a moment, the lights went out.

Angela had been impressed, when she had first seen the Marquis's Theatre, that he had installed electric light.

She knew, too, that it was in some parts of the house.

It made her think wistfully of how much electric light would improve the Priory.

The oil-lamps always needed attention, and the candles were dangerous.

Now there was a hush over the whole Theatre until, very slowly, the lights came up.

The curtain rose to show in the background the Debtors' Prison.

There was only just enough light to reveal several miserable-looking men, dressed in rags, sprawled on the ground.

The door of the prison was thrust open, and the Rake was pushed in by a Warder.

He was no longer smart, and there was an expression of despair on his face.

It was as if he knew he had lost his freedom and might even die behind prison bars.

He walked restlessly backwards and forwards, as if trying to find some way of escape.

Then two of the other occupants of the cell swore at him for keeping them awake.

He sank down on the ground in abject despair.

As he did so, he gasped, as if he were dying, but nobody paid him any attention.

Finally, he fell back as if unconscious or dead.

It was then, with a brilliant light, behind her, that Angela came in very slowly from the farther corner of the prison.

She walked towards the Rake, and stood for a moment, looking down at him with compassion.

He raised himself and spoke in a voice of anguish.

He asked how could he have been such a fool as to have lost his life in this ridiculous fashion?

She told him in a soft voice that she had come to give him another chance.

If he repented of the mess he had made of his life and for all the foolish things he had done, he could do better another time.

"Another time?" he asked. "Are you really telling me that I can live my life again?"

Very quietly Angela replied:

> "You will come back—come back again
> As the red earth rolls.
> God never wasted a leaf or a tree.
> Why should he squander souls?"

The way she spoke was very moving.

She had, in fact, never heard the verse until the Marquis told it to her.

She had asked then:

"Did you write that?"

He shook his head.

"No, I would like to have done, but actually, it was written by a friend of mine called Rudyard Kipling."

Now, as she finished speaking, the whole audience was absolutely silent.

The Marquis, raised on one arm, was looking at her.

She held out her hand.

"Come," she said, "and when you come back with your talents and no debts, you will, I know, do better than you have done this time."

The Marquis grasped her hand.

As he rose, the light flowed in brilliantly to make her presence seem dazzling.

The Orchestra broke into chords of celestial music which seemed to carry everyone listening up into the sky.

Then, slowly, the curtain fell.

For a moment there was only the silence which every actor knows is the greatest tribute an audience can pay him.

Then there were cheers as the audience rose spontaneously to clap and go on clapping.

They were still cheering as the curtain rose and all the performers stood on the small stage.

Magnificent bouquets were handed to the women and a present from the Marquis was given to all the men.

Only when the Marquis ordered the curtain to fall was the performance really over.

It had not taken very long.

Yet Angela thought it was something that a great number of people would remember and think about for a long time.

It was then, still wearing their stage costumes, that they went into the Dining-Room.

Instead of one long table, small ones had been placed around the room.

Names had been placed on a number of them.

Angela was delighted to find that she was sitting with Trevor and Sadie Vandebilt.

With them, too, was a very charming man who had arrived from India only two days before.

"The one thing I have been thinking about as I came home," he said to Angela, "was the Marquis's horses, and when I rode one to-day in the Steeple-Chase, I felt as if all my dreams had come true!"

"That is how I felt when he allowed me to ride *Saracen*," Angela admitted.

She was aware, as she was talking, that Lord Grentham was looking at her from another table.

He was with one of the Gaiety Girls who had her ardent admirer beside her.

Angela thought Lord Grentham was looking frustrated.

She was therefore careful not to look in his direction again in case he came over to speak to her.

After the excitement of the Play, everybody seemed to be drinking more than they had the previous night.

The newcomers who had been in the audience were as noisy as the rest.

The women, Angela thought, were outrageous.

Two of them, when dinner was ended, wanted to dance on the tables.

They were prevented from doing so only because the Marquis objected.

"I must say," Sadie Vandebilt remarked, "I was

not expecting English people to behave like this!"

"The answer to that is," Trevor explained, "that this is not the sort of party you would normally be expected to attend."

"I guessed that," Sadie replied, "when Cousin Shaun was so astonished to see me and not, I thought, very welcoming."

"This is a party for his men-friends," Trevor explained, "and I think he contemplated sending you straight back to London."

Sadie laughed.

"I would refuse to go! Do not think I am shocked. I have seen worse things in New York and far worse at home, where they usually throw anyone who has had too much to drink into the swimming-pool!"

"That is something we do not have here," Trevor replied, "and it is too far to go to the lake."

Sadie laughed again.

"I would like to see some of these men struggling to the bank and looking like a lot of half-drowned rats!"

Trevor laughed.

It was then that one of the men got up from the table and, losing his balance, fell to the floor.

The Marquis rose, saying:

"I think we should all move to the Drawing-Room."

Trevor turned to Angela and said:

"Go to bed. Nobody will notice your absence, and if they do, I will make some excuse for you."

"And what will everybody else be doing?" Angela asked.

"Gambling," her brother replied curtly, "which is something I cannot afford to do. I intend therefore to suggest to Miss Vandebilt that I take her round the Picture Gallery."

There was a note in his voice which told Angela it was no imposition but something he wanted to do.

She therefore joined the crowd that was walking out of the Dining-Room.

When they reached the Hall, she slipped up the stairs.

She was half-way up, when Lord Grentham saw her.

"Where are you going, Angela?" he asked.

"To take off my wings," she replied.

"Shall I come and help you?" he asked.

She did not answer that, but hurried to her room.

She locked the door just in case he was impertinent enough to follow her.

She did not ring for the maid.

She had come up so early, it was unlikely Emily was expecting her.

Then she remembered that she had promised to go and see Lady Mary.

She took off her halo and her wings, and put on her dressing-gown.

As she did so, she looked at the clock.

They had been so long in the Dining-Room that it was now nearly midnight.

She was sure, therefore, that the child would be asleep.

At the same time, she felt she should keep her promise.

Unlocking the door, she peeped out and was

relieved to see the corridor was empty.

She hurried along it and there was no-one to see her as she slipped up the stairs to the Nursery floor.

She quietly opened the bedroom door, aware, as she did so, that there was a night-light burning.

Lady Mary sat up in bed.

"You have come! You have come!" she cried.

"I promised I would," Angela said, "but I hoped you had been a good girl and gone to sleep."

"How could I go to sleep when I was waiting for you?" Lady Mary asked.

Then, as Angela approached the bed, she exclaimed:

"Oh . . . you have taken off your wings!"

"Like you, I am going to bed," Angela replied.

Lady Mary held out her arms.

"Please . . . will you cuddle me and tell me a story?" she begged. "Daddy has not told me a story for ages and ages . . . and I would like to hear one!"

"I will tell you the story of Cinderella," Angela said.

As she spoke, she thought it might almost be a story about herself.

Then, because Lady Mary was holding on to her eagerly, she slipped into bed and put her arms round her.

"Once upon a time . . ." she began.

* * *

The Marquis, coming up to bed two hours later, was relieved to be rid of the noise made by his neighbouring guests as they drove away.

They had assured him, as they got into their carriages, that they had never enjoyed an evening more.

He noticed that Trevor and his cousin had disappeared.

He had been sure when he saw Angela going upstairs that she would not come down again.

Then he told himself that he wanted more than anything else to say good-night to Angela and thank her for playing her part so brilliantly.

There was no-one else he knew who could have looked so like an Angel and spoken like one.

She had moved the audience dramatically.

"She is a very remarkable young lady," he said.

He undressed, then opened the door of the *Boudoir* and walked across it.

It struck him that Brooke might be with her, in which case he must not intrude.

He stood outside the communicating door and listened.

He was sure, here was nobody with Angela.

Quietly he opened the door and looked in.

To his astonishment, the bed had not been slept in, although there was a small candelabrum alight beside it.

It seemed to him incredible that Angela would have broken one of the unwritten laws—that a woman never went to a man's bedroom.

He came to hers.

Because he was angry, the Marquis walked back across the *Boudoir* and, going into his bedroom, slammed the door behind him.

chapter six

ANGELA woke up and for a moment could not remember where she was.

Then she felt something soft and warm against her and realised it was Mary.

They had both fallen asleep while she was telling the story of Cinderella

The room was dark and the night-light had guttered away.

She thought, although she was not certain, that it must be about two o'clock in the morning.

Gently she moved Mary's head from her shoulder and slipped out of bed.

She tucked the child in.

Then, putting on her dressing-gown and slippers, she tip-toed across the room, closing the door behind her.

The corridor outside was dark.

It took her a long time to grope her way to the staircase.

When she got down to the next floor, there were still lights burning and she could see her way more clearly.

She went to her own room and was just about to take off her dressing-gown when she thought it was rather warm.

She pulled back the curtains and opened the window wide.

The moonlight turned the garden and the trees to silver, and they looked very beautiful.

She leaned out of the window to breathe in the cool air.

It was then she became aware that there was something strange to the left of her.

She looked towards it and saw to her astonishment a ladder rising from a vehicle up to the Second Floor.

She was wondering what it could be, when suddenly she saw a man appear out of a window.

As he was holding on to the ladder, another man placed something small and white on his back.

Angela stared at the bundle.

Then, like a flash of lightning, she knew what was happening.

She moved from the window, pulled open the door leading to the *Boudoir*, and ran across it.

She threw open the door of the Marquis's room.

His curtains were pulled back and she could see clearly that he was asleep in bed.

She rushed to the bed and shook his shoulder, saying:

"Wake up! Wake up! Mary is being kidnapped and there are men taking her down a ladder!"

The Marquis was instantly alert.

"What are you saying?" he asked.

"Hurry! Mary is being kidnapped!" Angela said breathlessly.

She turned and opened the door leading into the corridor, and ran out.

The Marquis jumped out of bed, thinking that Angela must be dreaming.

He went to the window and, looking out as Angela had done, saw his fire engine, which was a new acquisition.

Its ladder was resting against the sill of the Nursery window.

There was a man half-way down, carrying something on his back as a fireman would have done.

As the Marquis looked out, he could see a carriage which was drawn by two horses standing beside the fire engine.

A man held them while another waited to take the child he was carrying from the man on the ladder.

Even as he stared, the man on the ground took Mary from him and put her inside the carriage.

The Marquis looked up again and saw that a fourth man was coming down the ladder.

Then he saw Angela come running from the house.

Before the men realised what was happening, she had jumped into the carriage.

A moment later, as the fourth man reached it, the horses were already moving.

The man standing by the open door just had time to throw himself inside.

As it moved down the drive, he swung the door to.

The Marquis hurried to his wardrobe, threw on some trousers, then went to his chest-of-drawers for a shirt.

He then took a revolver from a small drawer and, dragging a coat from its hanger, he hurried across the corridor.

As he did so, he was deciding which of his friends would be sleeping alone.

He opened the bedroom door of the one who was nearest.

Just as Angela had done, he shook his friend by the shoulder, saying:

"Wake up, Harry! My daughter has been kidnapped! Meet me in the Hall as quickly as you can!"

He repeated the same words twice more before he ran down the stairs.

As he did so, the Night Footman, who was sitting in a padded chair near the front-door, rose to his feet.

"Run to the stables," the Marquis ordered, "and tell the grooms on night duty to saddle four of my fastest horses as quickly as they can!"

He did not wait for the surprised boy to reply, but hastened to the Gun-Room.

It was a room the Marquis's men-friends always admired.

There were shot-guns of every description, some very old duelling pistols, and several blunderbusses.

There was also a cannon which had been captured by one of the Vauxhall ancestors at the Battle of Waterloo.

The Marquis pulled open a drawer in which there was a number of revolvers.

He drew out three, two of which were up-to-date and one a little older.

He loaded them and carried them into the Hall.

Two of his friends had just reached the bottom of the stairs.

The third was not far behind and, as he handed out the revolvers, Harry asked:

"What has happened? How do you know she has been kidnapped?"

"I will tell you about it later," the Marquis said. "There is no time now! We have to try to intercept the carriage before it reaches the main road."

All four men ran to the stables.

Two of the horses were already saddled, and the grooms had nearly finished with the other two.

It was only a few minutes before the Marquis and his friends were riding down the drive.

"Those devils cannot go very fast in the lanes," the Marquis said grimly. "Follow me—we will go across country."

He set off as quickly as *Saracen* could carry him.

They jumped a number of hedges and made very good speed, keeping to the flat land, and where the fields had not been cultivated.

They must have ridden for nearly two miles before the Marquis saw what he thought was the top of the carriage.

It was moving along a twisting narrow lane.

He pointed it out to his friends without speaking, then set off at a gallop to get ahead of the carriage.

All four swept over a fence and landed safely in the lane.

The carriage came round the corner.

It took the driver a second or two to realise that two men on horseback were blocking the road.

The others were standing on the verge behind them.

He drew in his horses and, as he did so, the Marquis could see there were two other men besides him.

As he looked, the man on the outside put his hand inside his coat.

He had only half-pulled his revolver out, when Harry shot him in the arm.

He gave a shrill scream of pain.

* * *

When Angela had jumped into the carriage, she had found, as she expected, that Mary was gagged.

Her body was encircled by a rope.

She untied the gag.

Mary burst into tears.

"I'se frightened! I'se frightened!" she sobbed.

"Of course you are, Darling," Angela answered, "but I am here and I am sure very soon your Father will come and save you."

As she spoke, the carriage started to move.

The fourth man, who had been beside the door, jumped inside.

"Now then, wot be yer doin' 'ere?" he asked Angela.

"I might ask you the same question," she said, "but instead, I will ask you to please untie the rope round this child's ankles. It is far too tight."

"An' 'ave 'er 'runnin' away?" the man asked who had sat down on the seat opposite them. "Oi ain't doin' nothin' like that!"

The coach was swaying.

"How could we possibly run away?" Angela asked scornfully. "Why are we going so fast? Even if we tried, we would not get very far in our nightgowns."

As if the man thought what she said was funny, he laughed.

"Got an answer for everythin', 'aven't yer?" he answered. "Well, Oi s'pose it'll do no 'arm to tak' th' rope orf, but any trouble an' ye'll wish ye'd never bin born!"

Angela did not answer.

She watched as he undid the rope that was tied tightly round Mary's ankles.

Angela eased it over her arms until they were free.

Mary could then hold on to Angela and hide her face against her shoulder.

Angela stroked her hair.

"Now, you have got to be brave, as your Father would want you to be," she said, "and of course the little girls in the stories I am going to tell you were always very brave."

Mary looked up at her, her face wet with tears.

"You will tell me a story?"

"I will tell you lots of stories," Angela said, "and this will be an exciting one for you to tell when you get older."

"Those men came in," Mary exclaimed indignantly. "They put a handkerchief over my mouth and picked me up out of bed."

"I know," Angela said soothingly, "and it was very bad and wicked of them. When your Daddy finds out what they have done, they will be very sorry."

"That's wot you fink!" the man opposite them said. "But us wants a great deal o' money for this 'ere child 'fore we sends 'er back."

"I think it is very cruel of you to frighten anyone so small," Angela said, "but I have to admit it was clever of you to climb up to the window with that long ladder."

The man smirked.

"Oi 'eard as 'ow 'Is Nibs paid a pretty penny for that fire engine, an' it served our purpose right enough."

"It was a long, long ladder," Mary said, "and I thought he might drop me and I would fall on the ground."

"But you were not dropped and now you are quite safe with me," Angela said, "and as soon as we get to wherever we are going, I hope there will be somewhere comfortable where we can go to sleep."

"Oi dare say we c'n find ye a bed o' sorts," the man opposite said, "but Oi'm not sayin' it'll be as comfortable as wot yer're used to."

He was sneering at her, but Angela thought it would be a mistake to antagonise him.

"I am sure you are really kind-hearted," she said, "especially where it concerns small children. Have you any of your own?"

"Oi've got three," he answered, "an' they're more trouble than they're worth!"

"I do not believe that," Angela said. "You would not like your little daughter to be treated as you have treated this poor child."

"My gel ain' worth sixpence!" the man replied. "But this un's worth ten-thousand pound t'us."

"You will be lucky if you get it," Angela said quietly.

She realised they were now in the lanes and the carriage was forced to go slower.

She wanted to ask where they were going, but guessed it would be a long way from the Marquis's house—perhaps somewhere in London.

She could only say a prayer of thankfulness that she had seen what was happening.

She could not imagine how terrible it would have been for everybody to wake up in the morning to find that Mary's bed was empty.

There would be only the fire engine outside her window to show them the way she had been kidnapped.

Mary had stopped crying and was holding tightly on to Angela, as if she were still afraid.

"Now, suppose we start our story?" Angela said, smiling at her. "Once upon a time, there was a little girl called 'Mary.' She went up to bed after having had a happy day playing with her toys."

"Was that me?" Mary asked.

"That was you!" Angela replied. "She had no

idea that anything was going to happen during the night."

"You have forgotten about the Angel!" Mary interrupted. "An Angel came to see me with her wings on."

"Oh, yes, I had forgotten that, and she came back again without her wings to say 'good-night.' "

"The Angel should have known that something bad and wicked was going to happen," Mary said.

"Perhaps she did know," Angela said, "or else another Angel warned her, so that she looked out of her window and saw you being carried down the ladder."

"Did the Angel tell you it was me?" Mary asked.

"Yes, she did," Angela replied.

As she spoke, she realised that the horses were being pulled to a standstill.

Then there was the explosion of a shot being fired, followed by a scream.

The man opposite jumped to his feet and pulled down the window.

"It is your Daddy come to save you," Angela whispered.

As she did so, she saw the man put his hand into his coat pocket and pull out a large pistol.

He leaned out of the window.

She realised in horror that he was going to shoot at the Marquis.

With a swiftness born of fear, she sprang at him.

By catching hold of his arm with both her hands, she forced the pistol upwards.

He must have pulled the trigger, but the bullet went harmlessly up towards the sky.

As it did so, the Marquis turned and shot him through the shoulder.

The man dropped his pistol, and still leaning out of the window, clutched his wound with his other hand.

The Marquis slipped down from his horse and pulled the door open so that the man fell out onto the road.

He picked him up bodily and threw him into the ditch.

At the same time, Harry had pulled the man driving the horses from his seat and struck him with a blow on the chin.

It sent him to the ground unconscious.

The other man in the front of the carriage was treated in the same way by one of the Marquis's other friends.

Having disposed of the man he had shot in the shoulder, the Marquis put his head inside the carriage.

Mary, who was already on her feet, flung her arms round his neck.

"Daddy, Daddy, you've saved me!" Mary cried.

"Are you all right, my poppet?" the Marquis asked.

He looked at Angela as he spoke.

"We are all right," Angela answered, "but . . . rather frightened."

"It is all over now," the Marquis said, "and I will take you home."

He put Mary gently down on the seat.

"I will join you in a moment," he said.

He left the carriage to look with satisfaction at the

four kidnappers who were all lying in the ditch.

Two were groaning from their wounds, but the others were unable to speak.

"Are we going to leave them there?" Harry asked.

"They will find it a long way to walk to London, or to wherever it is they have to go," the Marquis replied. "You drive, Harry. Lionel and George can lead our horses back to Vaux."

"What do you intend to do with this dilapidated vehicle?" Harry asked as he climbed into the driving-seat.

"Keep it," the Marquis answered, "and hope that those devils hired it so that they will pay for it or go to prison!"

One of the Marquis's friends came across the road to take *Saracen*'s bridle.

"I am going to turn round," Harry said.

"You will find a place a little way up the road," the Marquis answered.

He got into the carriage as he spoke and sat down on the back seat between Mary and Angela.

As the carriage started to move, Mary cuddled against him.

Without saying anything, the Marquis put his arm round Angela as if to support her.

Because she was so relieved it was all over, she suddenly felt like bursting into tears as Mary had done.

It had been one thing to be brave while they were at the mercy of the kidnappers.

Now they were both safe and she felt weak and limp.

As the carriage swayed, she instinctively put her

head against the Marquis's shoulder.

"You must tell me what happened," he said, "but first of all, I want to know how you were aware of why Mary was being kidnapped?"

"I had just left her," Angela answered, "and gone back to my own room."

"Just left her?" the Marquis questioned.

"She was telling me a story, Daddy, about Cinderella," Mary said, "but we both fell asleep. When I woke up, the Angel had gone and those horrid men were putting a handkerchief over my mouth!"

"So you were with Mary!" the Marquis said as if he were speaking to himself.

"How could I have guessed when I left her that anything so horrible would happen to her?" Angela asked.

"You saw it from your bedroom window," the Marquis said as if he were trying to work out exactly what had happened.

"I could not believe it! I thought I must be dreaming!" Angela replied. "Then I came to you."

"That was very sensible of you," the Marquis said, "and it gave me the chance of preventing them from reaching the main highway."

"You saved us," Angela murmured, "and that is all that matters."

"I think, actually, it was you who saved Mary," the Marquis said, "and I am very, very grateful."

"She was just telling me a story," Mary told him, "about a little girl who was very brave. And that was me!"

"I can see you have been very brave," the Marquis said. "I am very proud of you."

"Really proud?"

"Very, very proud!" he answered. "And I shall have to find a medal to give you."

Mary gave a little cry of joy.

"A medal . . . like you have?"

"A much better one," the Marquis said.

Listening, Angela thought she had never expected him to be so understanding with his daughter.

She was sure it was a side of his character of which few people were aware.

They drove on, and she thought the most comfortable and reassuring thing she had ever known was the strength of his arms around her.

There was no need to talk, no need for explanations.

Mary was safe, and that was all that mattered.

Only as they were nearing Vaux did the Marquis say:

"I do not want either of you to talk about this to anybody! Do you understand, Mary? It must be kept a secret between you, Angela, and me, and I am going to tell the friends who helped me not to talk."

He thought for a moment.

Then he said:

"I expect you will want Trevor to know, but nobody else! If they did, everyone will have a great deal to say on the subject. If it becomes public knowledge, it might encourage other villains to try the same thing."

It was then Angela said:

"They were going to ask a ten-thousand-pound

ransom for your daughter."

"She is worth a great deal more than that to me," the Marquis remarked, "but it would be a great mistake to let anybody be aware of it."

Harry had turned the horses into the drive.

He was now bringing them to a standstill outside the front door.

The Marquis helped Angela and Mary out of the carriage.

"I will take the horses round to the stables," Harry offered as they walked up the steps.

There was only the Night Footman in the Hall, and as they made their way up the stairs, Mary said:

"I . . . I do not want to be . . . alone in my bed . . . in case those bad men . . . come back!"

"No, of course you do not," Angela agreed, "and you can come into my room for what is left of the night."

She looked at the Marquis as she spoke as if for his approval, and he nodded.

"It is something I wanted to suggest," he said, "but was not certain whether you would agree."

"Of course I want Mary with me," Angela answered, "and there will be no reason for us to be woken too early in the morning."

"I will see to it," the Marquis agreed.

She took Mary into her room and helped her into the big bed.

"I like sleeping with you," Mary said, "and when you wake up, perhaps you will tell me a story."

"I will do that," Angela said, "but first we must go to sleep, otherwise we shall be too tired and disagreeable to-morrow."

Mary laughed.

"Angels are never disagreeable!"

"And I do not believe they are often very tired," Angela replied.

The Marquis had disappeared for a moment.

Because she thought he might come back to say good-night, she quickly took off her dressing-gown and slipped into bed beside Mary.

She had only just pulled the sheet over them, when the Marquis returned.

"I have left a note to say that you are not to be disturbed," he said. "All you have to do when you are ready for breakfast is to ring the bell!"

"Thank you," Angela answered.

He looked down at Mary.

"Good-night, my poppet," he said, "and you are not to think about what happened to-night, because it is something I will take care never happens again!"

"But you saved me!" Mary said.

She put out her arms to the Marquis as she spoke, and he kissed her.

Then she snuggled down beside Angela and he stood looking down at them both.

Unexpectedly, he bent forward and kissed Angela gently on the lips.

It took her by surprise, and for a moment she could not believe it was happening.

It gave her a strange sensation she had never known before.

Then he raised his head.

"Good-night, and thank you," he said quietly.

Before she could realise what was happening, he had put out the light and left the room.

For a moment she could only lie there, thinking it was impossible to believe that she had been kissed for the first time in her life.

And by the Marquis.

She could still feel the touch of his lips on hers and the strange sensation it had evoked in her.

It was then she knew she loved him.

chapter seven

ANGELA awoke because somebody was pulling back the curtains.

At first she thought it was the maid who had failed to read the Marquis's note.

Then, as she opened her eyes, she realised it was Trevor.

He came and sat down on the bed facing her.

"I am sorry to wake you," he said, "but it is nearly half-past-ten and we are leaving at noon."

"L-leaving?" Angela asked.

They were speaking in low voices because Mary was fast asleep.

She had moved away from Angela during the night and was sleeping on the other side of the bed, her back towards them.

"The Marquis told me what happened," Trevor said, "and because I want to take Sadie to Tattersall's early to-morrow morning, I thought it a good idea that we three should leave immediately."

Angela did not reply, and he went on:

"The Marquis wants to keep what happened a secret from everyone in the house, but I think that sooner or later they will find out. It would be a great mistake for anyone, including the Marquis, to know who you are."

"Yes . . . of course," Angela agreed.

"Very well," Trevor said. "Get dressed. The Marquis is sending us back in the carriage that brought Sadie here."

He did not say any more, but went from the room.

Angela rang the bell and got out of bed.

The maid came hurrying in, and by that time Mary was awake.

She was taken upstairs to be dressed.

"Her Ladyship's got to go downstairs to see her father," Emily said. "He's waitin' for her in his Study."

"I want to be with Daddy!" she said. "I have lots to talk to him about."

As soon as she had gone, Angela put on the elegant gown she had worn to travel to Vaux.

Emily packed her things into the trunk she had brought with her.

At exactly five minutes to twelve she went downstairs.

She found Trevor with the Marquis in the Hall.

There was no sign of the Gaiety Girls or any of the rest of the party.

"Everybody else is sleeping late," Trevor said as if she had asked the question.

Angela did not answer.

She was looking at the Marquis and thinking how handsome he was.

At the same time, she was shy because he had kissed her.

When her eyes met his, she blushed.

Sadie came running down the stairs, seeming like a Spring wind sweeping through the Great Hall.

"Do not tell me I am late," she said before anyone could speak. "It is only one minute off twelve, and I almost killed myself to be ready in such a hurry!"

"You will be glad you made the effort when you see the horses I am planning to show you first thing to-morrow," Trevor said, "and after we have been to Tattersall's we will go to the country to inspect the Marquess of Northampton's stud."

He was speaking more to the Marquis than to Sadie.

The Marquis said:

"I heard that since Northampton inherited the title, he is selling off some of his Father's race-horses."

"I think they are exactly what Sadie wants," Trevor replied.

"I told you you would be in good hands!" the Marquis said to his cousin.

She kissed him.

"I agree you are right, and we will tell you all about it to-morrow evening."

The Marquis turned to Angela.

"You are all dining with me to-morrow," he said. "I am greatly looking forward to it."

There was something in the way he spoke the last

147

words which made Angela's heart turn over in her breast.

However, as she went down the steps to where the carriage was waiting, she knew that she would not be joining the party.

This was good-bye.

Sadie got into the carriage, and Angela held out her hand to the Marquis.

"I shall always remember your beautiful house," she said in a low voice.

"And I will never forget what you have done for me," the Marquis replied.

His fingers closed over her hand.

Then, as she stepped back into the carriage, he was saying good-bye to Trevor.

"Seven-thirty to-morrow evening, Brooke," he said, "and Sadie and I will be waiting for you."

"We will not be late," Trevor said.

He got into the carriage and sat between the two women.

"There is room for all of us on the back seat," he said firmly. "I dislike sitting with my back to the horses."

"So do I," Sadie replied. "It is strange how we both dislike the same things."

"It is more important that we should *like* the same," Trevor said quietly.

As they drove on, it would have been impossible for Angela not to realise that her brother and Sadie Vandebilt were talking in a very intimate manner.

Because she was still tired after what had happened last night, she went to sleep.

She awoke only when they stopped at a Posting-

Inn and had a late Luncheon.

They hurried over it.

When they set out once again, Angela took off her hat and shut her eyes.

She knew even if she did not sleep, it would be tactful.

But apart from that, she was in fact still very tired.

* * *

They reached London late in the afternoon and went first to the Marquis's house in Park Lane to drop Sadie off.

Angela's trunk had been placed on the carriage in which they were travelling.

She had learnt that the Courier and the lady's-maid who had escorted Sadie to Vaux were behind them in a brake.

Sadie said good-bye to Angela without leaving the carriage.

Then she said good-bye to Trevor, but Angela could not help over-hearing her say in a whisper:

"You will not be long?"

"I will come back, my Darling, as soon as I have taken care of Angela," Trevor answered.

As they drove off alone, Angela looked at her brother and he said:

"You must have guessed by now that I am very much in love."

"Oh, Trevor, how exciting," Angela exclaimed, "and she is so sweet!"

"She is the most adorable girl I have ever met in

my life, and I would marry her if she had not a penny to her name!"

Angela drew in her breath.

"Marry her? Do you really mean to say that you are going to marry Sadie Vandebilt?"

"As soon as we possibly can," Trevor confirmed. "She has first to tell her Father, and, as soon as I know that everything is all right, I will be going to America with her."

"Oh, Trevor, I do hope you will be very, very happy!" Angela said.

"I shall be," Trevor answered. "You realise, Angela, that this will solve all our problems?"

Angela looked at him, and he went on:

"I know that everyone will assume that I am marrying Sadie because she is rich, but when I suggested that it was embarrassing that she had so much and I have so little—she said: 'What does money matter—I have too much of it anyway!' "

Angela laughed.

"That is just what I would feel."

"She will be thrilled by the Priory," Trevor said, "and of course we can make it look just as it used to."

It was difficult for Angela to realise how everything had turned topsy-turvy when she had least expected it.

When they went to Trevor's Lodgings she asked:

"What about my clothes?"

"I will take them back to the Gaiety for you," he said. "The important thing now is that you should go home. And remember, you are to vanish and no-one must ever know that you were part of the party the Marquis gave for his men-friends."

Angela did not speak, and he went on:

"In a way, it would not be so bad if it were known that Sadie was there too, but she is not English. The gossips who would criticise me for using my sister in such a way would think she did not count because she is American."

Angela knew the situation was worrying him, and she therefore said:

"No-one need ever know what happened, and it is unlikely I shall ever meet again anyone who was there."

"I hope not, but anyway, they will have forgotten about it by the time I am married to Sadie and have had a long honeymoon. When we come back to England, we will cope with the Priory."

Trevor spoke as if he were planning it all out and added:

"What you might do, Angela, is to have the roof repaired. We have money in the Bank now, which will go a long way to keeping out the rain."

"I will do that," Angela answered.

As soon as they arrived, he sent Atkins to the Livery Stable to hire a Post-Chaise with two horses.

Angela was about to expostulate at the expense.

Then she remembered that in the future money would no longer be important.

"You will be quite safe on your own," Trevor said as if he were reassuring himself more than her.

"Of course . . . I shall," Angela answered.

She had sat down at her brother's desk while he was giving orders to Atkins and had written a note to the Marquis.

Now she gave it to Trevor, saying:

"Will you give this note to the Marquis? It is just to thank him for my visit and to explain that regrettably I cannot come to the dinner to-morrow evening, as I have to go to the country."

"That is sensible of you, old girl," Trevor said with satisfaction. "I will leave it at the house when I go back to be with Sadie."

There was only one thing Angela had to do now.

That was to change out of the gown she had been wearing and which belonged to the Gaiety Theatre.

Then she put on one of her own from out of the trunk she had left at Trevor's Lodgings.

Back in her old clothes she felt she was really Cinderella in her rags.

It was a simple, cheap little gown that made her, she thought, look very different.

By the time she was ready, Atkins had returned, saying that the Post-Chaise was outside.

Trevor inspected it and noted that the horses were fresh and young.

It should not take them more than an hour-and-a-half, he thought, to get Angela back to the Priory.

She kissed him affectionately, saying:

"I am so, so happy that you have found Sadie!"

"We fell in love the moment we saw each other," Trevor said. "I thought it was something that happened only in novels, but it certainly did to us!"

"I will look after everything," Angela promised, "and please . . . try to come and see me before you leave for America."

"Of course I will," Trevor said.

She thought, however, that he spoke rather too quickly.

There was every likelihood that he would be unable to do so.

She got into the Post-Chaise and waved to Trevor until he was out of sight.

Then, as she settled down for the journey ahead, she realised that her future was very bleak.

She could stay at the Priory until Trevor came to live there with his rich and beautiful Bride.

But they would certainly not want her, and the question was: where was she to go?

It was a depressing thought that she could not think of at the moment.

*　　*　　*

As the horses carried Angela up the drive, she saw the Priory ahead.

She thought despairingly that this was the house in which she had lived all her life.

Now it was no longer the place she could call her home.

"Where shall I go? Where . . . can I go?" she asked.

There was some satisfaction in knowing that the Higginses could now buy what food they wanted.

Also that the Builders could come to restore the roof.

At the same time, as she walked about the Priory, she could not help thinking of Vaux.

She thought of *Saracen* and how much she had enjoyed riding him.

However much she tried not to think of the Marquis, he was always there in her thoughts.

When she went to bed, it was impossible not to lie awake, thinking of the rapture she had known when he kissed her.

She could feel again that strange sensation in her breast.

"I love . . . him!" she told herself over and over again.

She knew that her love for him was as foolish as wishing she could fly into the sky or dive down into the depths of the Ocean.

She wondered if he would mind, when he arrived in London, that she was unable to dine with him.

He might find it an uncomfortable meal with Sadie and Trevor absorbed in each other.

But, as he had hundreds of friends there was no reason he should not take a dinner partner.

Angela found it very difficult to sleep that night.

All she could do was to lie awake, thinking of the Marquis.

She kept remembering how handsome he was, how smart, and how exciting it had been to be rescued by him.

He had put his arm around her in the coach.

"I love . . . him! I love . . . him!" she told the stars as she looked out of her window.

They made her think of the stars shining over the garden at Vaux.

She pulled the curtains to so as to shut them out.

* * *

The next day the Builders arrived and Angela explained to them exactly what was wanted.

They shook their heads and told her it was a long job and an expensive one.

However, she persuaded them to set to work straight away and they promised to come back the next day.

When they had left, the Priory was once again very quiet.

She moved around it, feeling as if it already no longer belonged to her.

The rooms in which she had played as a child and grown up had already slipped from her grasp.

She must leave them behind when she went down the drive to some unknown destination

She looked up at her Father's portrait over the Study mantelpiece.

'Help me, Papa,' she begged.

She felt there was no answer.

She walked along the wide corridor, as the Monks had once done, towards the Great Hall.

The door was open, and the rays of the sun were coming through it.

As she reached the Hall, she felt as if the Monks were still there, welcoming travellers and anyone else who needed their help.

Now it was she who needed their help.

She was just about to ask them for their blessing.

Suddenly she realised with a start that she was not alone.

She looked around and saw, standing in front of the huge Medieval fireplace, a man.

For a moment she thought she must be dreaming, or else imagining what she saw.

But, as her eyes met the Marquis's, she knew it was him.

For a second she could only stare at him, and neither of them moved.

Then he asked in a strange voice:

"How could you go away without telling me where you were going?"

"Why . . . why are you . . . here?" Angela asked.

A sudden throught struck her, and she exclaimed:

"Mary? She . . . is all . . . right?"

"Mary is safe," the Marquis answered. "But I am very hurt! I was extremely upset last night to learn that I could not get in touch with you."

There was a note of reproach in his voice that made Angela look away from him.

Then she asked:

"I . . . I am sure . . . Trevor did not . . . tell you . . . where to find . . . me."

"No. He said very convincingly that he had no idea where you were."

"B-but . . . you are . . . here?"

The Marquis smiled.

"I used my brain, as I am sure you would have expected me to."

"H-how did you . . . do that?"

"I went to Trevor's Lodgings to try to persuade him to be more helpful than he had been last night. He was not there, but his man-servant, Atkins, told me what I wanted to know."

"Atkins? But . . . he does not . . . know . . ." Angela stammered.

" . . . That Trevor is your brother!" the Marquis finished.

"You know that?"

"I guessed it when I learnt where you had gone, and that is why I came here."

Angela realised that Atkins would have told the Marquis where the Post-Chaise had been ordered to go.

But she had never imagined in her wildest dreams that the Marquis would follow her.

"I think now, you have a great deal of explaining to do!" the Marquis said firmly.

Angela clasped her hands together.

"Oh, please . . . please," she begged, "you must never tell . . . anyone that I . . . came to your . . . party and pretended to be a . . . sort of . . . Gaiety Girl . . . but I did it to : . . help Trevor save . . . the Priory."

"Save the Priory?" the Marquis questioned.

"W-we have no . . . money," Angela said simply. "The ceilings are falling in . . . the roof needs repairing, and . . . we could not . . . afford to . . . pay for the . . . food we were eating."

She looked up at him piteously.

"If it were . . . known that Trevor had . . . taken his . . . sister to . . . such a party . . . everyone would be very . . . shocked and it would . . . hurt him."

"After all you have done for me, I would never do anything that would hurt or upset you!" the Marquis assured her. "And that also applies to your brother."

"You will . . . keep it a . . . secret?" Angela said. "Oh, thank you . . . thank you! He was so . . . afraid

157

that we . . . would be found out."

"And now that I have found you out," the Marquis asked, "what are you going to do about me?"

She looked at him, not understanding.

Then there was an expression in his eyes that made her heart start beating frantically.

"I think," he said quietly, "you will have to make sure that I will not betray you, and the best way to do that is to be with me as I want you to be."

"I . . . I do not . . . understand," Angela whispered.

He went nearer to her.

"I am asking you to marry me, my Darling," he said. "Mary has begged me to bring you back to Vaux, and that is what I want to do."

He put his arm round her and pulled her close to him.

He could feel her trembling as he said:

"I think you love me a little, and it will be very exciting, my beautiful Angela, to teach you about love."

His lips touched hers, and Angela felt as if he carried her up into the sky.

She had no idea that anything could be as wonderful as the feelings he evoked in her.

He kissed her and went on kissing her, at first gently, then passionately.

She felt as if her body melted into his as his lips became more and more demanding, more and more passionate.

To Angela it was everything she had ever dreamt of, everything she had never expected to find.

It was so perfect, so wonderful, that all she could

158

think of was that she had left the Earth and reached Heaven.

As if the Marquis felt the same, he raised his head and said:

"How can you make me feel like this, my precious little Angel? I have been searching for you all my life but did not believe you really existed!"

"I . . . love you . . . I . . . love . . . you!" Angela whispered. "But . . . I never for a moment thought you would . . . love me."

"But I do love you," the Marquis said. "I knew it when you acted so brilliantly in my Play. Then, when you saved Mary, I knew that you were everything that mattered in my life, and I would not want to go on living without you."

"You . . . really want me to marry you?" Angela asked.

There was just a little hesitation before the Marquis said:

"I was afraid when you were deceiving me that it was something I would not be able to do because it would have shocked my family and friends. But now, my Darling, there are no obstacles, no difficulties, and I think we should both be very grateful for that, if nothing else!"

"It is . . . so wonderful that you . . . love me," Angela whispered.

He knew as she spoke that she did not understand the agonies he had been through.

He had thought she belonged to Trevor.

Now he knew that the Brooke Family was as old and revered as his own.

While the Priory was a perfect background for

the Bride that he would take with him to Vaux.

He pulled Angela suddenly closer against him as if he were afraid that even at the last moment she might somehow be lost to him.

"I love you with all my heart, and with all my soul, which I did not know I possessed until now," the Marquis said. "You are an Angel from Heaven and I know that my whole life has been changed because you are with me."

"You know . . . I have nothing to give you . . . but my . . . love," Angela said. "We were so very, very poor until George Edwardes gave Trevor a thousand pounds for finding an Angel to take Lucy's part. It seemed like . . . a fortune!"

The Marquis laughed.

"I suppose Edwardes paid so much because he was afraid I would refuse to finance his Show if he let me down over my Play. It was something I intended to do, anyway. And now, because it has brought you to me, I will double what I was going to give him!"

"It seemed a fortune," Angela said, "but now that Trevor is going to marry Sadie, I was . . . wondering . . . what was to . . . become of me . . . when I found . . . you in the Hall."

"What is going to happen now," the Marquis said, "is that you will marry me immediately. I cannot wait for you, Angela, and there are so many things we have to do together to make our lives as perfect as I intend them to be."

His lips moved over the softness of her skin as he said:

"There has always been something missing in my

life, but I was not certain what it was. Then, when I saw your perfect, exquisite little face, I knew in some strange way that Heaven had sent you to help me."

"Oh, Darling . . . you know I will . . . help you," Angela said, "but you will have to help me to do the right things. We have been so poor since Mama died, and I have never been to London, attended Balls, or been presented at Court. You must . . . help me not to . . . make mistakes."

She thought the sudden radiance in the Marquis's face was very moving.

"You are what I always wanted in my life," he said softly. "Someone completely unspoilt, someone who really is an Angel, not because of her looks, but for what is in her heart. My precious, I love you and adore you!"

He kissed her until they were both breathless.

Then he said:

"I am taking you with me now—immediately— to London!"

"To . . . London?" Angela questioned.

"You will stay with my Grandmother for two nights," the Marquis said, "while I buy you a wedding gown and anything else you need. We will be married in the Chapel at Vaux, then we will go on our honeymoon."

"I do not believe . . . this is . . . true," Angela said. "I am . . . dreaming and when I . . . wake up I shall find you have . . . disappeared."

"That is something that will never happen," the Marquis answered. "We will start our honeymoon by going to Paris, where I can buy you your trousseau. You are going to look, my precious one, exactly as you should. Not as a Gaiety Girl, not even an Angel, but mine from the top of your exquisite head to the toes of your tiny feet."

He swept her into his arms and kissed her.

As he did so, she thought that to dress her and make her look beautiful was something that would interest him.

Then she knew that all this was unimportant beside the fact that they loved each other.

Although some people might mock the idea, she was certain they had been together in other lives.

That was what she had told him when he was acting "The Rake."

She was a part of him as he was a part of her.

Their hearts, souls, and bodies had been joined as they would be joined together now, and again and again in the future.

As the Marquis's lips held hers captive, she found herself saying over and over again in her heart:

"Thank You . . . God . . . thank you! Please . . . make me the Angel he . . . believes me . . . to be."

ABOUT THE AUTHOR

Barbara Cartland, the world's most famous romantic novelist, who is also an historian, playwright, lecturer, political speaker and television personality, has now written over 575 books and sold over six hundred and twenty million copies all over the world.

She has also had many historical works published and has written four autobiographies as well as the biographies of her mother and that of her brother, Ronald Cartland, who was the first Member of Parliament to be killed in the last war. This book has a preface by Sir Winston Churchill and has just been republished with an introduction by Sir Arthur Bryant.

Love at the Helm, a novel written with the help and inspiration of the late Earl Mountbatten of Burma, Great Uncle of His Royal Highness, The Prince of Wales, is being sold for the Mountbatten Memorial Trust.

She has broken the world record for the last sixteen years by writing an average of twenty-three books a year. In the *Guinness Book of World Records* she is listed as the world's top-selling author.

Miss Cartland in 1987 sang an Album of Love Songs with the Royal Philharmonic Orchestra.

In private life Barbara Cartland, who is a Dame of the Order of St. John of Jerusalem and Chairman of the St. John Council in Hertfordshire, has fought for better conditions and salaries for Midwives and Nurses.

She championed the cause for the Elderly in 1956, invoking a Government Enquiry into the "Housing Condition of Old People."

In 1962 she had the Law of England changed so that Local Authorities had to provide camps for their own Gypsies. This has meant that since then thousands and thousands of Gypsy children have been able to go to School, which they had never been able to do in the past, as their caravans were moved every twenty-four hours by the Police.

There are now fifteen camps in Hertfordshire and Barbara Cartland has her own Romany Gypsy Camp called "Barbaraville" by the Gypsies.

Her designs "Decorating with Love" are being sold all over the U.S.A. and the National Home Fashions League made her, in 1981, "Woman of Achievement."

She is unique in that she was one and two in the Dalton list of Best Sellers, and one week had four books in the top twenty.

Barbara Cartland's book *Getting Older, Growing*

Younger has been published in Great Britain and the U.S.A. and her fifth cookery book, *The Romance of Food*, is now being used by the House of Commons.

In 1984 she received at Kennedy Airport America's Bishop Wright Air Industry Award for her contribution to the development of aviation. In 1931 she and two R.A.F. Officers thought of, and carried, the first aeroplane-towed glider airmail.

During the War she was Chief Lady Welfare Officer in Bedfordshire, looking after 20,000 Servicemen and -women. She thought of having a pool of Wedding Dresses at the War Office so a Service Bride could hire a gown for the day.

She bought 1,000 gowns without coupons for the A.T.S., the W.A.A.F.'s and the W.R.E.N.S. In 1945 Barbara Cartland received the Certificate of Merit from Eastern Command.

In 1964 Barbara Cartland founded the National Association for Health of which she is the President, as a front for all the Health Stores and for any product made as alternative medicine.

This is now a £65 million turnover a year, with one-third going in export.

In January 1968 she received *La Médeille de Vermeil de la Ville de Paris.* This is the highest award to be given in France by the City of Paris. She has sold 30 million books in France.

In March 1988 Barbara Cartland was asked by the Indian Government to open their Health Resort outside Delhi. This is almost the largest Health Resort in the world.

Barbara Cartland was received with great enthusiasm by her fans, who feted her at a reception in the City, and she received the gift of an embossed plate from the Government.

Barbara Cartland was made a Dame of the Order of the British Empire in the 1991 New Year's Honours List by Her Majesty, The Queen, for her contribution to Literature and also for her years of work for the community.

Dame Barbara has now written 575 books, the greatest number by a British author, passing the 564 books written by John Creasey.

AWARDS

1945   Received Certificate of Merit, Eastern Command, for being Welfare Officer to 5,000 troops in Bedfordshire.

1953   Made a Commander of the Order of St. John of Jerusalem. Invested by H.R.H. The Duke of Gloucester at Buckingham Palace.

1972   Invested as Dame of Grace of the Order of St. John in London by The Lord Prior, Lord Cacia.

1981   Received "Achiever of the Year" from the National Home Furnishing Association in Colorado Springs, U.S.A., for her designs for wallpaper and fabrics.

1984   Received Bishop Wright Air Industry Award at Kennedy Airport, for inventing the aeroplane-towed Glider.

1988   Received from Monsieur Chirac, The Prime Minister, The Gold Medal of the City of Paris, at the Hotel de la Ville, Paris, for selling 25 million books and giving a lot of employment.

1991   Invested as Dame of the Order of The British Empire, by H.M. The Queen at Buckingham Palace for her contribution to Literature.